THE BLACK RIVER PLAYERS

j. thomas richards

REDINK
PRESS

Thanks to:
Dolores—For unending support and love.
Carl Herzig—His notes and feedback on the early pages
were invaluable.
Tom Caufield—For re-igniting my love for the written
word.

Special thanks to:
Randy and J. Ford—Without their critiques, suggestions,
and enthusiasm, this book would never have seen the
light of day.

For Rain and Carol

PART ONE

───────────

THE DIRTY BIZ

1

On the eastern edge of town just beyond the last humming streetlight, Randy Lee Wise flipped his denim collar up against the October wind, and sauntered into Frank's Tap to kill the Grass brothers.

He'd been living the clean life—or thereabouts—as a dishwasher in an all night Louisville diner when Floyd, a brother from the stoney lonesome, called with the opportunity. According to Floyd, Leon Hutchins (whoever he was) and his boys were upright on the wrong side of gravel. Supposedly, this opening move would lead to bigger things—it'd change business in Black River and the seat was his, if he wanted the ride.

Randy Lee didn't have to think about an answer. It was the first time since getting out two years before he felt something beyond hate float through his veins. Two hours later, he was headed north on I-65.

Floyd set him up in an Airstream, a secluded vintage twenty-eight footer, with a wad of money and tweak, told him to keep a low profile 'til the go-ahead. Randy Lee settled in and burned through the money in seven days Then eight more weeks passed with no word. He occupied his time with Black River's extracurricular, made friendly with some locals, and cooked a few batches of Nazi cold to see him through. He grew restless—penciled Floyd down on his shitlist—ready to throw in the towel and head home when he finally got the green light.

Inside Frank's, a modern country tune wafted from a juke against the back wall. The song didn't speak to him any. This new garbage sounded like it was recorded inside a computer or something—might as well have been a droning refrigerator. Give him some Hank—now *that* was red-blooded American music. Mama used to spin those LPs back when he was in cloth diapers and a wooden highchair.

The bar was dead except for Georgie Boy (surprisingly bigger than he expected) and some nigger wannabe barely old enough to be there. They huddled at the dartboard left of the entrance and shot him a look on his way to the bar. He just flashed a buttery yellow grin, gave a thumbs up. Randy Lee thought the kid was probably a plaything the way Georgie Boy carried on, giggling and tossing his darts all limp-wristed. Disgusting.

The whole country was knee deep in shit.

Used to be they hid their sickness. Now these sodomites walked around in broad daylight, giving the mongoloid and primitive races a run for their money. They were everywhere, spreading their cancer like plague rats. You couldn't go to the gas station or the commode without one trying to nail you in the ass. And if they weren't trying to bang you, they were trying with your kids.

When the proprietor, Frank, didn't acknowledge him, Randy Lee rapped the bar top and shouted in his

Kentucky drawl, "Hey hoss—you mind?"

Frank glanced up from the sink and set aside the glass he was washing, dried his hands on a towel, and walked over to the stranger. He rested both hands on the bar. "I can serve you one, buddy—then you gotta go. Last call was five minutes ago."

Randy Lee edged onto a stool. Behind him Georgie Boy and the kid resumed their dart game. He glared back at Frank.

"All right. Gimme a Coors, sir," he said, a malicious undercurrent beneath his courtly manner.

Frank spun around and pulled a can from the reach-in, set it on the bar. "Two fifty," he said.

Randy Lee slapped down a five. "Go ahead and keep it."

"Thank you kindly," Frank replied, not looking at the man as he swiped the bill into the register.

"How long you been here then?" Randy Lee asked. He cracked open the beer, slammed half.

"Oh . . . ten years or so."

"Ain't too much business, huh?"

"Not at ten to three on a Tuesday."

"Shit, this when the night's just gettin' interesting."

Georgie Boy came up beside him, nodded for another drink. Frank refilled his pint glass.

"Thought it was last call?" Randy Lee asked.

"Friend of the bartender, buddy," Georgie Boy said.

Randy Lee felt him eyeball the SS Runes inked on his neck. "Well, I am sorry," he said, turning to the brother. "You'll have to forgive me. New to town."

3

"For sure," Georgie Boy said. "Seems you took a wrong turn somewhere."

"Georgie Boy," Frank cautioned.

"Yeah, Georgie Boy, who kicked sand in yer pussy? Why don't you go back to tossing your darts." The two men stared at each other for a tense moment. Then Randy Lee forced a cackle and slapped Georgie Boy on the shoulder. "Awww, man . . . I'm just fuckin' wit ya, Georgie Boy! You guys er good shit."

"That's just fine," Frank said. "Hurry your drink along and be on your way."

"All right. I really do 'preciate it. Like I says, I just got into town. Here fer a bit helping a friend. First time to Iowa. I like it." Randy Lee finished his beer and wiped his mouth with the back of his hand. "Buuuuut . . . I suppose you're right. It's late. Mind if I use your pisser?"

Frank motioned with his head toward the back. "All the way down and to the left."

Randy Lee hopped off the stool with a clap of his hands, and winked at the kid as he marched to the back. Maybe it was the three days without sleep, or the nine weeks of pent-up aggression waiting for this night, or maybe it was just his fractious disposition, but in the bathroom, he unzipped and pissed on the floor, giggling in the high-pitched register of a delinquent seven-year-old. Then, satisfied with his handiwork, he took a Luger from the back of his jeans, cocked it, and shoved it into his front jacket pocket.

When Randy Lee reappeared, Georgie Boy was still at the bar, whispering to his brother.

"What's that now?" Randy Lee said as he stepped back to his place at the bar.

4

"Who'd you say your friend was?" Georgie Boy asked. "I wanna make sure I let im know we ran into you."

Randy Lee chuckled. "Nah, you wouldn't know him."

"I'm sure I do, friend."

"I ain't yer goddamned friend." Randy Lee drew the Luger and fired into Georgie Boy's temple.

His body hit the floor. His pint glass shattered. Frank auto-piloted toward his piece at the other end of the bar. Randy Lee aimed and unloaded three into the barkeep's chest before he made it four steps.

The kid lunged out the door like his feet were on fire. Sensing movement in his peripheral, Randy Lee rotated and fired blind. The shot splintered the plywood paneling.

Randy Lee hurried out after him. The kid ran east into the dark cover of the residential area. Randy Lee halted in the middle of the brick road, and fired off another round. At first, he was certain the shot connected, but then he glimpsed the kid's oversized white T-shirt just before it disappeared.

"I'll see you again, schoolboy," Randy Lee yelled into the cool air.

Big Deal's heart rattled against his ribcage. If it was true he'd deny it, but he wouldn't be surprised to discover a log in his drawers. Something in his bowels gave way when he heard the shot whiz past, but he couldn't be sure—felt like he showered in his clothes.

A block from Frank's, his shriveled tobacco-

5

stained lungs were shot, but by then the adrenaline had taken over enough to push him through the rest of the way home. If he wasn't so exhausted, he might have been proud.

By the time he reached his front door, the stitch at his side had him nauseous and heaving. Even after ten minutes pacing his place with his arms over head, he shook ferociously and gasped for air. He tried to play it cool in front of Brandi, and initially she thought he was just spun to kingdom come, but the cat finally burst from outta the bag when, leaning over his wobbly knees to catch his breath, he'd puked—all Miller High Life and yellow stomach bile—onto the living room rug.

She tore into him and then went off to the kitchen to grab a bucket and wash cloth.

He rushed into the bathroom, locked the door, and splashed cold water over his face. He collapsed on the edge of the tub and fought back tears. It was futile—soon he was sobbing into his T-shirt, snot running down into his mouth. Brandi must have heard him; she banged away at the door, hollering again.

"Leave me alone! I'm droppin' a deuce," he yelled.

Big Deal just wanted to shut it off, but the scene at the bar was on a loop in his mind. The way that 'billy just came outta the bathroom and blasted Georgie Boy right in the temple. He shut his eyes, but it only clarified the horror. Over the years, he'd lied about it more than once, even bragged about it, but in truth he had never seen anybody get dropped like that. And if he was being completely honest, he'd never seen a dead body. Not even at a funeral.

His hands were shaking. He needed something to

calm the nerves. He jumped up from the tub, and went over to the mirror.

"You're Tony fuckin' Montana," he repeated over and over to himself.

At about the twenty-third time through, he remembered the half blunt he and Georgie Boy had smoked behind Frank's, and fished the rest from his pocket—all bent to hell like that freak Roland's gnarly fingers.

"It'd do just fine," he said out loud, and he smoked it in front of the mirror, repeating his mantra between hits. Brandi would be pissed—it was the last of their shit—but she'd have to fend for herself. He had bigger problems.

A slow-motion bubble formed around his head as he finished off the blunt, but it didn't stop his shaking. He dug out his phone, and with a trembling thumb, called Leon.

No answer.

When it went to voicemail after the tenth ring, Big Deal swore and felt another wave of tears bubbling under the surface. He reminded himself to take it slow, to sound out each word, but at the beep it poured from him all at once like his puke onto the rug. "Yo, Leon, where you at, man? All fucked . . . Frank and Georgie Boy . . . dead . . . really dead, man. I ain't playing. Suh . . . some 'billy. Come on, Leon, pick up the phone . . . Georgie Boy took one point blank to the head an . . . an . . . then Frank. We was there playin' darts. Dude saw me, Leon. He saw me and shot at me and I got the fuck outta there. Call me back."

He killed the call and stared into the mirror.

7

"You're Tony fuckin' Montana . . . hard as steel . . . Tony fuckin' Montana."

2

Across town, off Route 13 running north to Hegemony, in a motel room he paid for by the hour, William Wolfe leaned against the shower wall and kneaded his temple with both thumbs, hot water rushing over him in the dark, and wishing he'd passed on Ms. Fromme's offer for another bump.

The migraines always started as soreness at the base of his skull, and while the time it took to intensify to their zenith varied, they spread up and around his head, like a dense fog that obscured all other sensations and rendered time incomprehensible. Headaches were a daily discomfort of William's adult life, but it wasn't until a few years before, back in Chicago when things went to shit, that they became severe enough to schedule a doctor's appointment. They took his blood pressure, drew blood and sent a sample of it to the lab, even strapped him down for an MRI. None of it led to answers. After hours of waiting and tests, the doctor could only prescribe him muscle relaxers and usher him to the lobby with a referral for physical therapy. The pills made him nauseous and drowsy. He never bothered with the PT. Eventually, the migraines disappeared. For awhile.

The hot water and steam helped to loosen things up and he stood there motionless, letting it hit him in the face.

When the water turned cold, he fumbled to find the faucet and then, blindly raking the plastic curtain aside with his forearm, he stepped out of the shower and flipped the switch. The light buzzed and flickered for an instant and a clinical fluorescent white replaced the darkness, rousing a sharp pain beneath his eyes. Tiny spots of light materialized in his vision, dissolved, and rematerialized.

Then, the familiar sensation of an ice pick chiseling through his sinus passages returned. He cursed and jabbed a thumb into the corner of his nose.

Bzzzt.

Nerves tingled beneath cheek flesh.

For some reason, it instantly evoked memories of summer nights on his parent's farm. He'd lie in bed and fall asleep to the bug zapper out on the patio, counting insects as the device's two thousand volts sprayed their guts into the dark. During the humid season, crisp June bug carcasses cluttered the patio concrete, their shells crunching beneath his tennis shoes every time he ran in and out of the house.

He snatched a ratty towel with frayed corners from the rack above the toilet and dried himself. Afterward, he hopped back into his pants and eased into a wifebeater. He swayed, slightly off balance, toward the door.

He palmed the door knob, ready to turn it, when he registered peripheral movement that broke off the brain command before it reached muscle. Instead, his heart hit the gas and a surge of terror sped through him. He withdrew his fingers and spun left toward an amorphous shape.

It was his reflection in the steamed mirror.

He cursed himself. It'd be a long night if he was becoming paranoid of his shadow.

He tended to avoid mirrors—couldn't remember the last time he glanced in one—but it held him in its grasp and tractor beamed him closer. Without conscious intent, he wiped away the condensation that obscured his mug and knelt on the sink, his nose an inch from the glass.

The world twirled out of focus behind him.

All vices aside, there'd always been a dislocation between William's body and mind. Some of his first childhood memories were in front of his mother's bedroom mirror, overwhelmed with what he could only now articulate as a kind of vertigo of pondering. If he stared long enough, focusing wholly on his little brown irises, the thin scrim of reality would peel away. In those moments, he was both inside his body and completely free from it. Yet, he was neither. He wasn't there at all—reason and being nothing more than smoke dispersed on a soporific wind. Of course, it scared the shit out of him. How could true revelation not? More than once it brought him to tears, and sent him running to his mother yelling, "I'm alive—aren't I? I don't wanna disappear into nothing!"

Staring intently into the mirror of the motel bathroom, William felt the rumblings of that old panic, that absolute loneliness. No good could come from dallying with those thoughts. He concentrated harder on

11

his face and scanned the pores, hairs, and blemishes with microscopic precision, transforming into a Zen-like self-grooming automaton. A product of a Mexican-American mother and a father's muddy puddle of Caucasian, William had inherited Sara's fallow-toned skin, but, within the last two years, his thirty-six year old complexion had depleted to a clammy corpse white. He pulled at its post-apocalyptic geography, methodically sifting the outskirts, where acne and a few tweak lesions hovered like outlaws in wait.

Then the ice pick was back at it, answered with another thumb to the face.

Bzzzt.

He dug deeper the third time.

Bzzzzzt.

It stung but it seemed to help, like pushing an internal release valve.

He walked his fingers down to his mouth and stretched his lips away from his nicotine-stained teeth.

Nicotine. The word ended whatever spell the mirror held over him.

William stepped back from the mirror, hit the switch, and swung open the door. A violent sensory overload struck him upon entering the room and he almost retreated back into the bathroom. On the TV, Wile E. Coyote and the Road Runner were locked into their eternal psycho drama at a hundred and twenty decibels. At the same time, an mp3 player vied for aural territory from Ms. Fromme's portable speaker system. A noise complaint was just what he needed. He could already see the manager dialing the rotary phone behind the front desk. Hell, a squad car was probably burning down Route 13 now, red lights cutting into the night. Soon they'd be kicking in the door. He wondered how he'd explain it all to Hollis.

He wouldn't, that's how.

Ms. Fromme sat cross-legged at a wall, drawing concentric circles in various shades of lipstick. The contents of her purse were scattered across the floor.

"Four years later," she hollered, looking from the wall. How she knew he was there, he did not know, but for a moment her words seemed plausible. It seemed years had passed since he had abandoned Ms. Fromme for the shower. He flashed on himself as some tweaked out Rip Van Winkle vaulted away inside the motel bathroom while civilizations rose and fell.

He went to the window, peeked out the shade. The back of the motel was a dark field. No sirens. No men with riflescopes hidden in the brush. At least, not that he could see.

"Don't start with that," she said.

"Can you please turn that shit off?" William mumbled without turning from the window.

"Which one?"

"Both." But he didn't wait for her to respond and swung away from the window to the TV himself. One last 'meep meep' escaped before he shut it off.

"Aww . . . I love that show."

"I'll tell you how it ends." His voice shot through the room as she killed the music.

She mocked him with a frowny face.

William had met Ms. Fromme one night after bar close. On a head full of whiskey and tweak, he found himself in south Black River, where all the zombies stalked the night. She was working the corner of 2nd and Cooper, out front of the Bargain Barn (or what was left of it). She strutted up to his window in a hot pink mini and a screen printed kitty cat stretched across her chest, gold glitter eye shadow, ready to rock n roll.

William grabbed the whiskey bottle from the nightstand, took a shot. Then he marched to the chair at the corner table, and wrestled a pack of smokes and a bottle of Icy Hot from his front jacket pocket. He unscrewed the blue cap, dipped in his middle finger, and rubbed the balm under both eyes and the sides of his nostrils. In the time it took to light a cigarette, his eyes began to water.

"Doesn't that burn?" she asked. She leaned back on her elbows with her legs stretched out in front of her. Her knees twitched and bobbed like a child that had been stuck inside too long.

"Like hellfire." He wiped the excess on the back of his neck, replaced the cap, and went and lied on the bed.

"Why you do it then?"

"I get these headaches," he said, fighting the urge to run back to the bathroom sink and douse his eyes with cold water. "If you ride it out, it'll sometimes burn em from your mind."

Situating onto his back, William noticed a horror on the bathroom door, some nightmarish Muppet sketched in lipstick. He planked the cigarette in the ashtray and closed his eyes. "Please don't paint the walls. I have to pay for shit like that."

"It's a portrait of you." Ms. Fromme inched onto the other side of bed—an immense plateau of blanket between them. She took a cigarette from the nightstand and lit it, turning to her side and resting her head on her hand. She was doing something weird with her feet that shook the bed. He tried to block it out.

She stared at William for a long moment. "Don't you like how I look? I mean . . . it's just that you're payin' anyway. I'd almost do you for free. I mean . . . once, like, on the house or whatever. Most of em I have to tune out. You know, they're mostly my grandpa's age with their old man balls flapping against me. It's gross. It's like getting fucked by death, ya know? Sometimes I just wanna throw up." Ms. Fromme furrowed her mouth and exhaled toward the ceiling. "Honestly, sometimes I can smell the death on them."

Her eyes followed the smoke.

William was somewhere else—a dozen thought lines, all of them rocketing in separate directions at a thousand miles per hour from the hotel room.

The muted TV glowed in the dark room. Ms. Fromme snored from bed, skin slick with sweat. She twitched sporadically, still speeding along in dreams. William adjusted his watch and stepped to the nightstand. He placed a roll of money on the Gideon and shrugged into his jacket.

He left the room, and made his way down the second floor walkway. He descended the stairs and crossed the gravel parking lot to his car. A cool gust passed through the black oaks that lined the property, their leaves ruffling lightly like an ephemeral wind chime. He paused at the driver side door and eyed the dark field beyond the hotel.

William had chain smoked the entire fifteen minute drive back into town, and by the time he unlocked the apartment door, his migraine had rebounded to life. He staggered into the living room, not bothering to turn on the light, and knocked over a stretch of empty booze bottles left on the floor. He continued on undaunted through unpacked boxes until he toppled over onto the couch. A sudden bout of nausea hit him. His head bobbled above the coffee table, and he blinked mindlessly at the piles of cigarette butts that overflowed from the ashtrays. When the desire to vomit passed, he blindly pawed at his jacket pocket for cigarettes.

It took several tries to finally find the opening, but all the effort had been in vain. He unintentionally pulled out his badge wallet instead, and after realizing his mistake, tossed it to the coffee table. It collided into another bottle, spilling its contents of backwashed rum and cigarette butts.

He stayed there, leaning halfway off the couch with his head drooped to one side, occasionally grumbling in lobotomized gibberish.

At some point, he yelled, "Bzzzzzzt!" into the quiet.

Then in the last hours before dawn, he kicked off his shoes and ditched his pants in the hallway on the path to the bathroom shower.

3

Sheriff Hollis Fry grunted as he shifted his two hundred and sixty pounds out from the behind the wheel of the police jeep and into the nine a.m. sun. He tipped his hat to the curious neighbors clustered across the street from Frank's. A few greeted him with a mumbled "Sheriff" and accompanying nod. Though it sounded closer to a question, it was reassuring some folks still associated the hat with authority and respect. Both were hard to come by. Every day, it seemed, a piece of the place he loved broke off and got flushed down the shitter. He hardly recognized it. Almost forgot it ever existed. The Black River of his youth had simply evaporated like morning dew on prairie grass. Once neighbors helped each other, weathered hard seasons with integrity, waved when you drove past, filled church pews and didn't mow their lawns on a Sunday. Now if neighbors bothered to look you in the eye at all, it was with peepers glazed in paranoia or malice.

Sheriff Fry had been there when feds raided IMP ten years before, detaining three hundred undocumented workers. Most received five months for identity theft and were then deported. Their trials rallied an immigrants' rights group that demanded accountability for managers and chief executive shitheel Sheldon Harris, who, it seemed, had skimmed Sinclair's *The Jungle* when he drafted a business plan. The Iowa Labor Commission filed charges six months after the raid—nine thousand misdemeanor violations of child labor laws and a ten million fine for wage violations. The feds alleged he also supplied illegal workers false documentation. After a brief manhunt, they found Sheldon on a hotel floor outside Hegemony, a shotgun blowjob to the brain.

Since then, Black River gasped for breath like a middleweight past his prime. Where once corn was the imminent crop, plague labs sprouted from the soil. At last census, population count was at 6,784. Sheriff Fry was certain seventy percent were infected with tweak.

He pigeon-toed passed several squad cars and an ambulance on his way into the bar. The boys from the EMS team hovered over Georgie Boy's body. Sheriff Fry grumbled in acknowledgment and took stock of the room. "Where's City?" he said, adjusting his belt beneath his belly. One of the EMS team flicked his head to indicate beyond the bar. Glass crunched under his cowboy boots as Sheriff John Wayned passed the teak countertop.

William Wolfe, eyes shielded by sunglasses, squatted above Frank Grass' bloody chest. Damn kid looked a mess, probably slept in his suit. One side of his shirt dangled over his pants like a colostomy bag. Frank looked more presentable.

"Robbery?" Sheriff asked.

"Don't look it. There's two hundred in the register." William walked toward the Sheriff. "Ah . . .

18

looks like four people were here." He squeezed by Sheriff back into the front of the house.

"How you figure?"

William rummaged in his front jacket pocket and produced a bottle of saline solution, which he sprayed up each nostril.

Sheriff had phoned City's former police chief the day he interviewed six months back. There was a long pause on the other end, then the chief stumbled around for a few seconds only to state they relieved William from duty due to 'psychological distress.' Not a ringing endorsement. But Sheriff had no other options— detectives weren't exactly lining up to join Shit Town Police Force. The town was stretched thin already with the seven officers they had and the position's modest salary enticed few.

Beyond that, he'd known Sara and Lionel since high school. She was getting worse from what he'd heard. Maybe William had returned to help out at the farm. Mexicans had been in Iowa since shortly after the turn of the century, but Sara Basantes—as she was known back then—was the first he knew personally. Sheriff had spent his teens and twenties dreaming about what her chestnut skin felt like. Sometimes, after a few rare hits from Jhonnie Walker, the old yearning returned and he found his mind playing 'what if.' Hiring the prodigal son in her hour of need was the least he could do for her. He just hoped William didn't turn out to be more trouble than he was worth. Sheriff had enough on his plate. Two more years at most and he'd have enough saved to retire to Montana, maybe get a small plot of land away from a world he understood less every day, take up fly fishing.

19

William sniffed and rubbed the sides of his nose. "We got the big guy's pint glass all over the floor. That can's probably the killer's—it being roughly where the shooter'd be firing. We wiped it for DNA and prints." William swung around to the corner. "Over here by the dartboard's another half drunk pint glass."

"Okay, our boys here and two killers?"

"Maybe, there's two sets of darts. But there's a ring of condensation on that table—from a pint glass, not a can. My guess is Georgie Boy was shootin' darts with a friend when the shooter came in. Maybe he knew him, maybe not, but something brings him over to the bar." William raised his hands holding an imaginary gun. "Maybe there's an argument between the killer and Frank and Georgie Boy comes up for backup. Regardless, sonuvabitch blasts him in the temple."

"Then three into Frank."

William swung his invisible gun toward the hole in the wood paneling. "Yeah—and this is what makes me think there was only one shooter—he turns and misses, like he fired at a fourth one on the way out the door. We got a list of Georgie Boy's associates?"

"Nearly every scumbag in town," Sheriff Fry snorted. "But we'll have to look at some of the younger wildlife. Georgie Boy had a penchant for lost boys, if you know what I mean."

The two men stepped out into the sunlight.

"Don't think anybody's gonna be crying over their loss. Grass brothers weren't exactly contributing members of the Black River community—both of em been in and out of prison since they slithered out their mama's twat."

William stared at the crowd across the street.

"You talk with neighbors?" Sheriff asked.

"Yeah. Nada. A blast of gunfire at three in morning and nobody calls the police?"

Sheriff Fry grunted and hooked a thumb into his belt.

William patted the outside of various pockets. Then, as if remembering where they were, he dug his cigarettes from the breast pocket of his jacket and lit one. A gloom drifted from his nostrils over his shoulder like a weightless scarf. "You gonna release the crime scene? I could use some breakfast."

"Yeah, good work." Sheriff Fry stared into William's dark sunglasses. "How you holdin' up otherwise?"

William flashed a devil grin, biting down on his cigarette butt. "I feel like a million bucks."

"Really? Cuz you look like shit, son. How's your mama?"

But William had pivoted toward downtown, smoke trailing behind him.

"All right . . . Well, at least run a comb across your head before leaving the house," Sheriff called after him. William Wolfe was a little soft in the frontal lobe for sure, he though- before turning back to the bar.

William slumped over the counter of the Ballyhoo Diner, trying to concentrate on the laminated menu. He couldn't tell if Hollis Fry was a super-friendly sort or just suspicious. Either way, he'd have to watch himself around the Sheriff. Honestly, he needed to get his shit together, but that was a constant refrain that had been running in his head since Chicago. The florescent lights buzzed incessantly in his ear. He rubbed his eyelids—the insides were like sandpaper—and peered over his shoulder. Hungry locals packed the place—the voices and chiming silverware made him edgy and a bit lightheaded. The facial landscape of the diner seemed to bear down on him all at once and something like shame passed through him. For a second William feared everyone in the diner knew he was high and whispered his transgressions over their omelets and pancakes ("Doris, you see the new detective's on the meth? Shame—his mother losing her mind and all. When do think he slept last? Somebody should tell the Sheriff. Pass me the salt, would ya?"). He chewed the inside of his lip. An odd sensation of bi-location washed over him. He was both there at the Ballyhoo counter and a million miles away on some astral plane.

A horrible cackle broke out, kicking his heart into overdrive. Jesus! The whole world was ending. He spun back toward the counter. An automaton face sculpted in foam-rubber features hung on the wall. Articulated eyelids blinked as its witchy glass eyes shot back and forth in unison with a lower jaw that howled out the top of the hour. Seeing it, he remembered his parents had brought him here once as a child. The geriatric face had been so intensely frightening, William refused to return.

"Need a refill, Sunshine?" The waitress asked, holding up a pot of coffee. She didn't wait for a reply and filled his cup. "You ready then or do you still need more time?"

"Ah . . . I'll take the French Toast Combo."

"How you want them eggs?"

"Scrambled. Please."

"Sausage links or bacon?"

"Neither . . ."

She glanced up from her notepad.

". . . I'm vegetarian."

"How you gonna get full, you don't eat meat?"

"I'll just take another egg if that's okay." He gnawed at his lip.

She shrugged her eyebrows. "Fine by me—I ain't eatin' it," she said and broke away toward the kitchen.

To William's left, a seven-year-old rolled a small metal fire truck around his plate of pancakes. He looked over at William and smiled.

The last time William saw his son, he'd taken him to a movie. As the credits rolled on the superhero flick, the two sat in the middle of the empty theater. The boy always demanded they stay to the very end. He wanted to see everything.

"Hey, Dad," his son had said, eyes glued to the screen.

"Yeah?"

"I love you."

The unsolicited declaration caught William off-guard and he fought back a surge of emotion. "I love you too."

"Dad," his son said, his eyes still not moving from the credits.

"Yeah?" William's voice wavered.

"I wish you could live at our house with mom and me. And you could wake up there and play cars with me." He kicked his little feet back and forth under the seat.

William hadn't known how to respond and wiped at his face.

23

After a moment he said, "I know. Me too."

William waved back to the boy with the metal fire truck. His father, a thickly bearded man in his forties, scowled at William with red hot eyes. William nodded back but the man's look didn't soften as he shoveled a fork load of sausage into his mouth.

William turned away and fumbled in his pockets until he located his Klonopin bottle. He loosened the cap and laid a pill on the counter. Then he split it with his knife, downed half with a swig of coffee, dropped the other half back into the bottle, retightened the cap and shoved it back into his jacket.

Robert Crimley walked with his son, Carson, to their pickup in the Ballyhoo parking lot. At the driver side, he unlocked and opened the door, playfully slapping Carson on the bottom.

"Get your seatbelt on," he said, scratching at his beard.

"I know." Carson crawled over to the passenger seat, reached up, and yanked the belt across his chest.

Robert got in behind the wheel. He plucked a toothpick from the box on the dash and made a sucking sound as he forced it into the cracks of his teeth. Breakfast sat heavy in his stomach. He leaned forward and let a high-pitched sigh escape his bowels. Carson looked at him and laughed, cracking his window.

"You think we can do some shootin' today?"

Robert stared out the window. "Oh, I don't know. We'll see." He dug the keys from his jeans. As he started the truck, he glanced down at the fuel gauge. It was on E. "Goddamn it."

Carson eyed him, curiously. "What?"

"Nothing."

Money had been tight since he lost his job at the factory. He really shouldn't have been taking his son out to eat, but it was a minor indulgence. Soon it wouldn't matter. He threw his arm over the seat, and reversed out of the parking space. They came to the end of the lot. The new detective, the one who had sat next to them inside, had exited the Ballyhoo and was crossing the sidewalk. He turned his head, eyes wet and pink, and waved. Robert didn't return the gesture. Who was that guy kidding? He was a drug-addict.

"Who's that?"

"Some scumbag."

"Why's he a scumbag?"

But Robert didn't answer. When the detective passed, he pressed the gas, and the truck roared out of the parking lot onto the street.

4

Roland Jarzenbowski shuffled along the curb of Brown Deer Road with a black hoodie draped over his face. A pickup honked as it whizzed by and the driver yelled, "Get outta the road, freak!" Roland, oblivious to the demand, continued on with slightly palsied steps.

It had been a good day but he'd suffer for it later. His gnarled body already ached. The sun stabbed his eyes even behind the sunglasses. He'd spent the morning in the Pump N Dump and restaurant dumpsters on Warren Ave digging for aluminum cans and plastic bottles. He scored big behind JJ Auto and Muffler, where he discovered a recycling bin.

After four hours, he had lugged his garbage bags across town to Milde's General Store to redeem the spoils—nearly twenty dollars. Then, at the Rock Bottom, Ray and Delilah had paid him five dollars to sweep cigarette butts from the front and back of the bar. He pocketed about a dozen half-smoked cigarettes and another dozen contained enough tobacco to salvage and re-roll.

For anybody else, except maybe the octogenarians from Good Samaritan, the walk from Brown Deer to

Murdoch took five minutes. It took Roland twice the time, sometimes longer. Usually he didn't mind—he appreciated nature more now than he ever had before the fire—but the itch had grown from passing notion to fixation since he left Rock Bottom forty minutes before, expanding in his mind like a white balloon slowly filling with helium. Now it blocked out every other thought and need, and clamored to be satiated.

He turned right on Murdoch toward his mother's house. Mrs. Caufield, raking leaves off her sidewalk, avoided eye contact when he passed. A Mensa member and churchy to the core, she'd always been an uppity bitch anyway.

His appearance didn't change that.

At his mother's door, Roland grabbed the key from his pocket. The fire had burned away his fingers, melted down the flesh and bone like Crayolas in an oven, leaving discordant stubs in their wake. His least damaged, the right hand forefinger (and therefore his favorite, which, being a film buff, he christened "Polanski"), almost extended the entire length of the Proximal Phalange. He squeezed the key between his thumb and Polanski. Tasks that required small articulation were a bitch, but all in all, adapting to the limited maneuverability wasn't so bad. His constant twitch, on the other hand, made everything more difficult, and it took him three attempts to slide the key into the lock.

TV talk show laughter pierced his ear as he entered the house. Three cats trotted into the hallway to greet him. The gray tabby sniffed his scarred hand, but when he reached to pet her, she darted away into the house. Roland proceeded down the hall, past the living room where his mother watched TV from a recliner.

"Roland?" she said.

The other two cats scurried after him into the kitchen. Unwashed dishes, caked with rotten food bits, filled the sink. Abandoned convenience food boxes and crumbs lined the counters, as if a starving mob had raided the cupboards. Against the rear wall, four trash bags reeked enough that Roland, even with his diminished sense of smell, gagged. A brown puddle formed under one of them. He couldn't remember the last time he took out the garbage—maybe a month. His ma never did shit. He'd get to it later.

"Doris called awhile ago. She was walkin' Shelby over there by Frank's this morning. Said there was police. An ambulance took away two bodies."

Roland opened the refrigerator and hooked a Mountain Dew from the bottom shelf. The cats meowed at his combat boots.

"Why would I—I don't—I dunno anything about it, ma." Roland set the soda can on the table and went to the pantry. The cats followed.

In the living room, Roland's mother coughed into a balled-up tissue and sucked on a Virginia Slim in her other hand. She tossed the tissue onto an end table littered with medication. "That one you used to run around with back in school was over there on the scene, she said. I guess he's been back for awhile now. I didn't know that—never thought he'd be back here." She lowered her voice, "Always thought he was so much better than everybody else." Then she hollered back into the kitchen, "Did you know he's back in town, Rollie?"

The pantry floor was thinly strewn with litter and

dried cat turds. The litter box was a week or two past needing to be changed. The ammonia stink almost overpowered the smell of the trash. Roland buried his face in his shoulder and poured a cup of Purina into the cats' dishes. Then he returned to the kitchen and grabbed his soda. He opened a door next to the refrigerator.

"Huh, Roland? You know that?"

"I don't know—Dunno anything about it, ma."

Roland secured the door behind him and stomped down to the basement. Like the kitchen, his room was a trash heap of soda cans, beer bottles, porn, dirty laundry piles, CDs, LPs, comic books, DVDs, empty packs of cigarettes, and junk food wrappers. In a corner decorated with local gig posters, a beat up Les Paul leaned against a Marshall half-stack.

Roland plopped on the couch and yanked back the hoodie. Burn scars covered his head—irritated pink and blanched flesh swirled in opposite directions. Craggy blotches and pockmarks patched together like freshly hoed soil. His left auricle was melted down to an exposed hole. Only a few thin tuffs of hair remained on his scalp.

He snatched up an old cordless from the coffee table and, using Polanski, tapped in Biscuits' number.

"Yeah?" Biscuits said, answering on the fourth ring.

"Charlie, it's Rol—it's Roland."

"Uh huh. Yeah. I know. What's up? Kinda busy."

"I was just wonderin'—I scored some scratch— You gonna—err—I got enough for a quarter."

"Yeah, man. I'll be here."

"Well, I mean—could you—like, would you mind pickin'—stoppin' by and grabbin' me?"

"I dunno, man. I don't think I can leave the house right now. I'll have somethin' tomorrow."

"Huh?"

"Yeah, man, come by tomorrow."

Biscuits hung up.

Roland dropped the phone and hopped up from the couch. He turned on the stereo and pressed play. A thrash band blasted from the speakers.

He returned to the couch and fished a small bag from the debris on the coffee table.

Using all his stumpy fingers, Roland sprinkled the powder from the bag onto a piece of foil. He located an empty pen tube and stuck it in his mouth, pinched one end of the foil and lifted it from the table. With his other hand, he raised a lighter to the underside of the foil and, using what used to be his thumb, struck the flint several times until the flame took. He siphoned smoke up the tube into his mouth.

Roland relaxed into the couch and exhaled. It had been a productive day. A relieved smile crept to the corner of his mouth.

William spent the afternoon tracking down Georgie Boy's younger associates. Lee Mack was down in juvenile detention for assaulting his stepmom. Troy Canon flipped burgers at a pub and grub on Warren Ave. Of course, neither had seen or heard anything. Hadn't talked to Grass in weeks. Wouldn't know why anybody'd have beef with him. But word from both was that Georgie Boy had taken Norman Eckel, a kid known around town as Big Deal, under his wing.

William paid Norman a visit at his house.

A deflated basketball, skateboard, and rusted weight bench decorated Big Deal's yard. Nobody had mowed the grass all season. Various materials covered the windows: wood panels, duct tape, Styrofoam, and blankets stained in what looked like piss, shit, blood, and cum.

The kid was fidgety when he answered the door and let William in. He paced the living room a couple of times and then tried to sit down in a chair, only to get back up seconds later to fetch his smokes.

"You seem a little on edge," William said after Big Deal sat down again.

"Nah, man, I'm not on edge. Just get a little uncomfortable when cops stop by my house."

"Could it be that you were at Frank's when the Grass brothers got popped?"

"Nah, man. I wasn't there."

"Now both of us know that's a lie."

"I ain't lyin'."

"Come on now. Your prints were on a pint glass." William was the one lying now. They didn't find shit on the glass.

"Wha?" Big Deal's face turned red.

"You're a shitty liar, kid. You can start tellin' me the truth or we can go ahead and have this conversation at the station."

Big Deal cracked his knuckles nervously. "A'ight. I was there . . . but . . . I left early. I got home by ten. I swear."

"Why do I feel like you're still lyin'?"

"Dawg, my girl can vouch for me." Big Deal

threw up his hands. He looked like he was about to piss his pants. Or cry.

William didn't need spider-sense to know the kid knew more than he was telling. He pushed for more, but didn't get anywhere. He didn't think the kid was involved, but intuition told him he was the fourth guy in the bar. Looking to shoot holes in his story, William left the house and drove two counties east to the megastore where Big Deal's girlfriend, Brandi, stocked shelves. The trip turned out to be fruitless. She corroborated his story.

He opted for the scenic route back to Black River.

At a stop sign within county lines, William rifled through a pile of CDs on the passenger seat. He opened a few cases (Iggy and the Stooges, the Misfits, Leonard Cohen, Howlin' Wolf) and, not finding what he was looking for, tossed them aside. Inside Slayer's *South of Heaven*, he discovered the CDR with *Transforming Feelings with Mindfulness: Guided Buddhist Meditation for Beginners* chicken-scratched in Sharpie. He slid it into the stereo.

A car honked behind him.

He checked the rearview mirror then raised a left arm out the window to acknowledge the driver, and turned onto the rural highway.

There was a brief warning to not listen to the audio program while operating heavy machinery or driving, followed by three strikes on a deep bell, and then a voice drifted from the speakers with a nurturing authority. "May I be peaceful, happy, and light in mind and body. May I be free from anxiety, affliction, and anger."

William sped along the road. Beyond a stretch of foxtail and bur bristlegrass, a field barn sat on a bluff.

Cows grazed brown grass upon the muddy hillside. He furrowed his nose at the ripe scent of their shit wafting through the window.

"May I be free from attachment and aversion, mindful to avoid indifference. May I learn to identify and see the sources of anger, craving, and delusion within myself."

As William traveled on, he tried to concentrate on the voice, to allow it to re-center his mind and clear it of all thought of the past and the future. He tried only to inhale and exhale the present moment. He wanted nothing more than to just be in the present moment. But along the highway he passed cornfields that swayed in a gentle breeze and austere mobile homes that elicited a vague free-floating melancholia within him, and he felt a deep well of longing rise up and pull at him like teeth tearing at fat on bone.

He turned onto Foster Road and traveled some time before passing the abandoned IMP meat-packing plant—a wraithlike shadow on the outskirts of town. He crossed the iron bridge over Black River into the town's heart, and continued along its arteries of empty residential streets, boarded up businesses, bars and churches. He cruised by the middle school and the high school football field, turned on Fourth and drove by Mike's Antiques, the video store, the Pretty Penny, and rounded Grover Circle's quaint gazebo and fiberglass street lamps.

The police station was on a dead end just off Fourth. William parked in the lot.

"May I be able to identify and touch the seeds of joy and happiness within myself," the voice chanted before William killed the engine.

33

He reached into the backseat and retrieved a plastic bag. After he spoke with Brandi, William had wandered over to the toy department. He purchased a few action figures and a Lego set to send the boy.

William got out and slammed the door, ambled into the soot-ridden building with the bag in hand.

5

Forty-five miles north, Leon Hutchins swung his spider legs out the passenger side of a black SUV onto the Hegemony Airport parking lot and ran a hand through his receding hairline. He kept it long and slightly feathered on the sides like crow's wings. Perhaps Leon had been handsome once, but that was long ago—gravity had since gone to work on his oblong face, spurred on by decades of endless nights, and his jowls were beginning to droop. Light pockmarks etched his thin cheeks above an impeccably maintained horseshoe mustache. He was more force of nature than man and he moved with a kind of sleaze-chic posturing, like the spirit of rock n roll past its prime, the imaginary cameras of a private GQ shoot constantly upon him, disco collar unbuttoned to a gold necklace mingled with chest hair, Elvis' pelvis itching to get loose inside his pinstriped suit pants. Leon wore haggard like the banal and less dangerous wore Gucci—it looked good on 'im.

Between drags on a cigarette, he shook off the cool morning breeze, waiting for Carlos to finish parking. He hated mornings—the fact that he hadn't slept in five days didn't help his mood—and he hated playing errand boy even more but Queenie demanded his presence on this one. He knew better than to protest.

Carlos slammed the driver's side door and joined Leon, who shrugged his eyebrows, grunted—more at the world than his associate—and then swaggered across the parking lot toward the terminal entrance. His eyes circled the perimeter and landed on his companion who was able to keep the pace of Leon's long gait. 'El Negro' was scrawled in ghetto cursive across the left side of Carlos' neck. And he took that shit serious—black suit, black shirt, black tie. Leon often wondered if the daily uniform was the same suit or if Carlos had a closet full of them.

The Mexican, at least three decades younger, was a gift from California a few years before. Queenie's own bodyguard. Leon hadn't known what the sicario was capable of at the time—all newcomers and outsiders were suspect in his world—and he'd guessed the ink was over-compensation for something small downstairs. But virtually raised by Los Zetas, Carlos earned the moniker through the sheer brutality which he dispensed opposition. By fifteen, he'd witnessed, or was responsible for, more violence than most people saw in a lifetime watching cable.

Leon's opinion of Carlos changed shortly after his arrival. The two were coming back from California with a carload of product when a State Trooper stopped them in Nevada. The deputy sauntered up to the car with a shit-eating grin and Carlos blasted him through the window before he could even ask for license and registration. Then the young Mexican jumped from the car and dragged the body back to the squad. With the officer in the trunk, he stole the car. Leon followed him out into

36

the desert where they doused the interior with gasoline and watched it burn.

Reaching the automatic doors, Leon sucked one last drag before he flicked his cigarette and ground it into the pavement with his Chelsea boot, winking at a security guard as they entered the building.

The two men jaunted from the check-in lobby to the arrivals/departures board to make sure the flight was on time. From there they ventured past the gift shop into the concourse—the only concourse in Hegemony Airport—toward the greeting area. Along the way, Leon clocked a nubile blonde in a business mini. She bent over for something in a carry-on, her smooth legs throwing her ass up into the air, and he spied the lace-trim contour of her purple panties. She continued digging in her bag, right in the middle of the concourse, her ass hanging there like plump fruit on a carnal vine, ripe for the picking. Leon fought an urge to lurch forward and take a chunk out one of her cheeks. Leon was an ass man. Always had been. Dark meat, white meat, brown meat, yellow meat. It didn't matter. It was better than chicken. He could eat that shit all day. He continued to ogle as they passed her, a corner of his lip twitched as a surge rippled from his lower spine to his balls and, without consciously willing it, a scene involving her in the airport bathroom looped in his head.

Once they reached the greeting area, Carlos hovered to the window and stared out at the runway with his arms crossed. Leon claimed an empty seat—legs spread, arms up on the chairs around him. He was still adrift in his bathroom fantasy (going to town like a fat kid at a pie eating contest) when he felt a pair of eyes on him

37

and zoomed in on the other side of the seating area. An old woman in orthopedic shoes. He glared back until she returned to the crossword on her lap. Leon fell back into himself, tracing the shape of the blonde's labia in his mind.

Twenty minutes later his phone rang. He sighed and scooped it from his umber leather.

"Fuckin' twit," Leon said, looking at the caller ID. Big Deal.

He'd called over ten times in the last two days and left as many voicemails. Not that Leon had bothered to listen to them. Obviously, the kid looked up to him (who didn't?) but Leon was beginning to think he had an obsessed fan. The handful of times he'd been around him, the kid hung on his every word with that stupefied glaze over his face, saying shit like "Fo' sho" and "True dat, Leon!" or "Hey—hey—Leon you need a refill? Lemme buy you a drink—huh?" Huh Leon? Huh?

For fuck's sake. The kid bathed in his ball sweat. It was like Big Deal wanted to fuck him. Georgie Boy may have welcomed that kind of attention—Leon wasn't the kind to rain on another perv's parade—but he didn't have time, or slightest interest, in learning the puppy or basking in his street fame. Now maybe if the kid had a nice pair of tits and a big ol' onion things would be different. Besides, as green as this kid was, he'd definitely be the first to roll if shit ever hit the fan. Big Deal shouldn't have been calling at all. There was a chain of command to these things and shit bird was the lowest rung. Leon had only allowed Georgie Boy to pass along his number in case of an emergency.

He'd speak to Georgie Boy—set the kid straight.

But then again maybe it was wiser to cut the kid loose. Tuck him in. Put him to sleep. The kid was as hard as a ninety-year-old cock, and no amount of posturing could hide the fear in his eyes. Sure, that could translate to undying loyalty, but in Leon's experience, that kind of weakness was only a liability. A little lost puppy had no self-respect. He needed a home too badly. Leon wasn't his daddy.

He shook his head and muted the call.

Carlos double-clicked his tongue. Leon looked up. Out on the runway, the plane touched concrete.

Ten minutes later, the first passengers filtered out the exit ramp into the waiting area, their faces blurring together. Leon briefly wondered about their stories. Amazing they didn't fire a bullet into their thinker every morning when they woke up and looked into the bathroom mirror. Leon wasn't a man of reflection, but the thought of being trapped in their herd brains and missionary positions, made him feel as close to sadness as he ever got. Must be like living with a shotgun wound to the heart, quietly bleeding everywhere, imprisoned by inhibition and law.

Of course, it wasn't enough that they were living the American nightmare, they all wanted to procreate and make more bastards. Ultimately, it didn't mean shit to him, Leon was a lucky man. He had been gifted with an unwavering hand, and the soul of a king. He just wished they'd get the fuck out the way. They were taking up too much room in his rearview mirror.

A middle-aged man in glasses wandered from the crowd. Leon spotted him and whistled to Carlos, who turned from the window and nodded. Leon didn't move.

He just stared at the man until the man caught his gaze.

"Leon Hutchins?" the man asked as he approached.

Leon's eyes widened. "That'd be me."

He didn't smile.

"Daniel Hayes." When Leon didn't respond, Daniel turned to Carlos. "Yes, we've met before. Or, at least, I recognize you from your runs."

Carlos nodded.

"Well, now we're all here, let's get a move on. You're all she's been talkin' about for weeks. Wouldn't wanna keep her waiting," Leon said.

He jumped up and headed back toward the lobby without waiting for his companions.

Carlos steered the black SUV down a rural highway, a gravel cloud drifting up from the rear tires. Delicate hills opened to a stretch of flatland lined with Bur Oak. The three men traveled in silence, passing barren cornfields, dark soil littered in dead colorless husks. A few miles on, Carlos slowed and turned under an arched entry onto a long road to the compound.

In the back seat, Daniel—who had been looking out the window since they left the airport—finally spoke. "I wasn't expecting Iowa to be so gorgeous. There's sensuousness to the land. Like a woman's body—reminds me of a Neruda poem."

Leon, riding shotgun, raised his right eyebrow in bewilderment. They rolled past horse stables. "Just wait 'til you step out and smell the horseshit." Then, almost as an afterthought, he jabbed an elbow over the seat with a derisive smile. "But I'm glad we've exceeded your expectations."

"This place is huge." Daniel hadn't taken his eyes from the window.

"Three hundred and fifty acres."

Daniel glanced back at the stables. "So she's got a thing for horses?"

Leon scratched his horseshoe mustache. "Nah, I wouldn't say that."

Esmeralda Castillo sat with crossed legs, tapping her gel fingernails on the six thousand dollar designer desk in her office. A large print of the fire god, Xiutecuhtli—adorned in turquoise mosaic—hung between two bay windows behind her. The office overlooked the back of the compound. Just outside the window was the thirty-four foot pool, covered by a weather tarp, she had installed two summers before. Only the best. Seventeen K. Fiberglass. The hot tub would run through winter. She loved to loll in the effervescence as snow tumbled through the season's black nights onto her bare shoulders. The acreage beyond the deck—containing a large garden, bower, and three guest houses—disappeared into a grove on the property border. During days when she actually spent time in her office, she would often peer out on her domain, a smirk surfacing on her glossy lips.

It was a far cry from the two bedroom apartment she grew up in with her five siblings, and the beatings from Raúl. Moments like these were the only time she thought about her father. She wished she could bring him here, set him on his knees, and let him take in what he helped accomplish. In a way, she owed him everything. Preparing her for the world of men the way he did. She wondered if he'd be recognizable to her now. So much time had passed. So many things had changed. She imagined him hunched over and wary, maybe with a cane—if he was even still alive. Likewise, she doubted he'd recognize her. His 'Essie' wasn't so weak now, wasn't such an easy target.

There was a knock at the door.

Finally.

"Come in," she said.

Carlos pushed open the doors and entered with Leon and Daniel in tow. She stood up, straightened her skirt suit, and high heeled around the desk to greet them.

"Good morning. You must be the man we've been waiting for," she said, smiling at Daniel.

"Yes, indeed, I am. Daniel Hayes." He extended a hand.

"Pleasure to meet you," Esmeralda said and gently shook his hand, a bumblebee tattooed on her wrist.

"Pleasure's all mine. We're in awe of what you've managed to accomplish here—Antonio and Oscar have nothing but praise for you."

"Well, thank you. Aren't you sweet." She motioned her hand toward the furniture in the middle of the room. "Please . . . ."

Leon and Daniel sat on the couch. Esmeralda took the chaise lounge, and fingered her pearls. Leon sighed, fidgeting and repositioning himself, and leered out the bay windows.

"I take it your flight was suitable?" she asked.

42

"Yes, thank you. Oh, before I forget, Antonio wanted me to give you this." Daniel rummaged through the bag at his feet, pulled out a wine bottle, and handed it to her. "A small gift from his private stock."

"Oh, my—wonderful. We must absolutely open it this minute." She turned to Carlos. "Carlos, would you be a doll and grab some glasses?"

"Yes, Miss Castillo."

He strode to the cabinet on the far wall and returned with four glasses. Esmeralda filled each with wine and distributed them to the men.

Then pulling down the hem of her skirt, Esmeralda stood and beckoned the others to do the same.

She raised her glass. "To prosperous new beginnings."

In unison, the men responded, "To prosperous new beginnings."

Esmeralda, Leon, and Carlos drained their glasses. Daniel sipped his. Leon slapped him on the back and barked, "Well, you ready to do this shit, Vern?"

6

Miguel Rivera didn't go home when school got out. Instead he hoofed it beside Justin and Travis over damp yellow leaves to the Pump N Dump for an after-school Slurpee. None of them had money. If Eugene was working he'd let each of them have one on the house. He looked mean—his face all busted up with a crooked nose—but he was nice once you got to know him.

Unlike Benicio, who was the reason Miguel had started sleeping under the bridge during his stays. The man hadn't slept since showing up at the house a week earlier stinking of booze, and Miguel had learned it best to avoid him when he was on a binge. Benicio never liked him to begin with—told his mom she spoiled him, that he'd never be a proper man without some toughening up—but he was dangerous to be around when he had meth in him.

Miguel was convinced Benicio would eventually take it all the way and kill him.

The three boys shuffled into the gas station and went straight to the Slurpee machine in back.

"Gentleman, which way trouble blowin'?" Eugene said when they set their drinks on the counter.

44

They just smiled and shrugged.

"Well, best figure it out so you can cut the other way." Eugene grinned, showing off his gold-crowned canine. He glanced down at the drinks. "On the house. You know it. I gotta be good for something."

"Don't you get in trouble for giving us free stuff?" Travis asked, picking up his cup and sucking the straw.

"Sheeeiiit . . . look at this ugly mug . . . those dickless corporate fucks ain't gonna tell me shit."

The boys were still laughing a half block from the store. As they turned onto Brown Deer Road, Miguel wondered if Eugene could take Benicio. Maybe Benicio was tough against a twelve year old, but he wouldn't be shit against someone like Eugene. He'd probably get killed. Eugene was the biggest man he'd ever seen, while Benicio only stood a few heads taller than himself. The thought of Eugene pounding Benicio's head into the concrete put a smile on his face.

"What are you smiling about?" Justin said to Miguel after a pull from his drink.

"Prolly dreamin' about Mia Blinn," Travis said, causing Justin to chuckle.

"Whatever. You're the one's always staring at er skeeters in Ms. Starnes' class," Miguel shot back. The three boys laughed and continued down the road.

Within a week of meeting his mom, Benicio had taken over the house like an aggressive dog claimed new ground. He was always there, at least in the beginning, even the times she was at work. "Look, lil' bitch is here," he'd say from his spot on the couch, beer bottle between splayed legs, whenever Miguel came home. He was relieved when Benicio started disappearing for days, sometimes weeks, and Miguel fantasized, even prayed, the man would be mangled in a car crash or slowly bludgeoned to death with a blunt weapon outside a bar somewhere. But every time Miguel believed him gone for good, the bastard only came back, that violent look in his eyes.

One night the year before, after being MIA for a month, Benicio returned with his buddies. Miguel heard them laughing as he unlocked the front door and sneaked off to his room. He tried to stay there the whole night, busying himself with homework and a mystery book, but eventually hunger trumped wisdom and drove him to the kitchen. Smoke filled the room and the table was full of beer cans. Miguel eased around their party and went to the refrigerator. Benicio had just told a new one that was killing it, all of them busting a gut with big stupid smiles, but the man's face instantly tightened when he spotted Miguel.

"What you think you're doin', lil' bitch?" he said.

"I'm hungry," Miguel mumbled.

"Huh?" Benicio squinted and put two fingers on the back of his ear, "Can't hear you. Speak up."

"I'm just gettin' something to eat."

"Not there you're not. That's my food. You didn't ask if you could have any."

"I don't have to ask. My mom bought this food. This isn't even your house," Miguel snapped.

He regretted the words as they flew from his mouth.

"What'd you say to me?!" Benicio shot up from the table and slapped Miguel. "As far as you concerned, I own everything in your shitty little world. This is my

46

house. My kitchen. My food. Your ma's my bitch. You understand?"

Miguel, tears on his cheeks, nodded, looking at the floor.

"So you hungry?" Benicio said.

Miguel nodded again.

"Then you need to ask me if you can have some of my food."

Miguel hesitated, but then said, "Can I have some of your food?"

"Fuck no, that's human food. You eat lil' bitch food."

Benicio's friends squealed with glee back at the table. Seemingly encouraged by the laughter, Benicio yanked Miguel by the shirt over to the trash bin, and pointed to a casserole, thrown out two days before, layered with butts and ash and hair.

"That—that's your food."

Miguel pulled away, but Benicio forced his head into the trash. "No, no, no, you are hungry, you will eat."

Up until that point, Miguel realized, Benicio had just been gettin' his toe wet. After that night, the man's new passion in life was making him suffer. Miguel learned all kind of things over the next twelve months. How long cigarette burns took to heal. What Benicio's rhinestone-studded belt buckle felt like. How long he could go without pissing himself while locked in a closet.

Forty-six hours. Give or take.

He pleaded for his mother to kick Benicio to the curb, showed her the bruises and burns on his arms. She sighed, her brow bent in anger, "Why must you ruin my only chance at happiness?"

47

The boys neared the corner of Murdoch. Travis tugged on Justin's fleece and said, "This is the street he lives on."

"He does—which one?"

"That white one almost to the end there." Travis pointed.

"How do you know?" Justin's voice sounded doubtful. "I thought he was homeless."

"My uncle drove me by it the other night. He lives with his mom."

"Who're you talking about?" Miguel asked.

"That freaky crazy guy."

That didn't tell Miguel much. There were a lot of crazy people in Black River.

"You know, he's all melted and stuff." Travis said, contorting his face.

Miguel thought Travis looked more like a sad clown, but he knew who they meant. He'd never seen the man, only heard stories on the recess playground. Some had said he'd been burnt in a fire, others insisted he was born that way 'cuz his mom did meth, or that he worked at the meat-packing plant years ago and got mauled in some freak accident. Whatever the reason for his deformity, they all claimed he roamed the streets and alleys like a restless phantom.

"Hey, Miguel, I dare you to go knock on his front door," Justin said.

"Fuck no. I ain't goin' anywhere near that place."

Two blocks from Murdoch the boys hunkered down in Justin's living room to play Xbox, munching on Funyuns and passing a warm two liter of Mountain Dew between them. They had to take turns—in a fit of gamer's rage, Justin had smashed the second controller against the wall two weeks before—but Miguel didn't mind, he was just glad to play. Four months back, he came home to find that Benicio had stolen the console from his room and sold it to one of his loser friends.

A couple hours passed and Justin's mom traipsed in with some drunk glued to her side. Ms. Reynolds worked days at a downtown bar and sometimes she'd bring work home with her. The man struggled to keep the heavy lids of his bloodshot eyes open. At first, they seemed not to notice the boys, dropping onto one cushion of the couch. Drool ran down the side of the man's mouth like he had fallen asleep with it open on the ride over. He stared into Ms. Reynolds' eyes, inching his hand up her skirt, and burped out a few syllables only he understood. It was when he started to flap at her tig ole bitties, as Travis called them, that she glanced over and saw they were not alone.

"Oh, goddammit boys," she said, easing the man's hand away. "Time to play outside."

"But we barely got to play much," Justin protested.

"Get out now." The man fumbled again at her chest. "You need exercise 'stead of stayin' in all the time playin' that damn game."

It was dusk when the boys hit the cobblestone on Friendly Street. None of them discussed it, they simply drifted unconsciously toward Orville Levin Park—not so much synchronicity, but a lack of options. Some of the houses were so weathered with peeling paint and structural problems Miguel was surprised to see a light on inside. It was then, a few blocks down, he saw him.

49

A slouching silhouette ambled toward them, walking in the middle of the street.

Miguel paused as the gap between them and the shadow closed, causing Travis to look up. "Oh, shit. That's him!" His voice reverberated out into the quiet neighborhood.

They stood motionless and silent like the Universe hit pause on its remote.

When the shadow ventured from the gray of the coming night into the yellow pool under the street light, Miguel saw his damaged face. It was more monstrous than the stories made him out to be—both a demon summoned from their collective nightmares and, yet, something far more fragile and human.

The man flashed them a self-conscious smile.

They could only stand there, wide-eyed and awed—perhaps for the first time in their lives. Then he forged on into the night as a lonely October wind sent a few rogue leaves scuttling across the road.

Biscuits lived in a brick duplex. His neighbor was a nearly deaf blue hair who turned up her TV so loud there was a constant undercurrent of voices in Biscuits' place and, more than once, after a couple days of no sleep, Roland mistook them for spirits in the walls, shooting upright and cocking his head to the side to say, "Is that—what's—do you hear voic—can you hear people talkin'?" On the plus side, she couldn't hear for shit. And she never called the cops.

Roland pounded Biscuits' door.

On the fifth attempt, Biscuits shouted,

"Whaaaat?"

"It's me."

The door cracked open. Biscuits' glazed eye quickly peered out at Roland. Then he slammed the door and unlocked the chain.

"What up, handsome?" he said, opening the door wide to let Roland inside.

Biscuits was shirtless and had long brown hair. He looked exactly like JC, if JC had track marks and pipe burns on his lip. A rose encircled by Celtic thorns flanked his right shoulder, a scorpion the other. Both were a faded blue that bled into his anemic hue.

Years back, when Roland still had his mobile home, Biscuits had rushed over with one of his revelations. He was ecstatic about this idea for a back piece with Homer Simpson and Ned Flanders giving Marge the Eiffel Tower. He brought along a rudimentary sketch on a Pump N Dump napkin. When Roland said he could only see two Pac-men eating a hot dog, Biscuits became indignant and declared, "Well, I ain't an artist, man. You're the artist. I'm an ideas man. You gotta look past rough edges and see possibility." He ended up paying Roland in lines to work a drawing up to snuff. However, it had yet to materialize on his back.

Biscuits ushered Roland into the living room, adjusting his bomber hat and scratching at his cheek stubble. Disassembled innards of a stereo receiver were spread across the table. Biscuits had always been interested in electronics, but every now and again he'd hear a faint hum and would take apart everything with a cord looking for an FBI wire tap.

"What's up?" Biscuits asked, which really meant

51

"What do you need?"

"Erm—I got twenty." Roland pulled out a wad of ones and fives.

"All right." Biscuits grabbed the cash and counted it. Then he counted it again and shuttled off to his bedroom. He re-emerged five minutes later, slapped a bindle into Roland's palm, and yelled, "Bam!" as he did a little hop.

"Can I—do you mind if I—"

"Yeah, man, make yourself at home." Then as if getting shocked by a tweaker form of Satori he shouted, "Yo, let's do a poor boy!" and clapped his hands together.

Bingo.

St. Biscuits to the rescue.

Twenty minutes later, porn on the plasma screen, Roland leaned back into the couch as Biscuits fired a barrel into his mutilated arm. At once, all the aches in his body—tightness around his face, unrelenting headache, sharp throb at his extremities and complete exhaustion—left him. Simultaneously, the mixture of H and Ice projected him at warp speed through the ceiling, out into the cosmos, his constitution stretching away from his shipwrecked body like molasses toward exhilaration and transcendence.

But no matter how far Roland fled, his mind always returned to Rosemary.

7

William hunched over his fourth whiskey and coke—tie loosened, sleeves rolled up—and sensed a familiar supercilious stir somewhere around his heart. Having spent the day clenching his jaw, the muscles below his ears were tense enough to snap. He'd chewed the inside of his cheeks raw, but no matter how tender they became, he couldn't stop gnawing at the damn things.

Clearly, he reasoned, his bones suffered an undiagnosed claustrophobia that wanted to spring from the confines of his skin. He flashed on himself at the bar ripping open the flesh from his chest, his skeleton shedding loose skin like Clark Kent at costume change, before grabbing his glass again. He smiled off the image, shifting in his seat, but fought a potent urge to break from the bar and run screaming through downtown.

Unconsciously, William dug a thumbnail into the tip of his ring finger. He grunted, gnashing his teeth again, and looked down at a small blood droplet. He sighed, drained his drink, and forced himself to focus on the TV behind the bar. Fuckin' NASCAR. He swayed languidly toward a man two empty stools away, swinging an arm over the back of his stool.

"Hey, buddy, you watchin' this shit?" William heard himself say.

The man was engrossed in the countertop video game at the end of the bar, jabbing his fingers at the touchscreen. Without looking at William, he glanced up at the TV, shrugged a shoulder, and returned to his game.

"Jerry, can I get the thing?" William pantomimed thumbing a clicker.

The bartender walked over.

"Lewis," he said and handed William the remote.

"Yeah, right, right. Whatever." William examined the buttons. "How you work this?"

"Here." Lewis took back the remote and switched the channel to the news.

"Nah, Lewis, we can't abide this either."

"It stays."

"Well, could you at least refill my Crown and brown?" William jingled the ice in his glass.

Lewis poured him another drink and placed it on a fresh napkin.

"Thank you, sir." William handed him three ones. "Keep it."

According to the news, another black-clad teenager had opened fire on a food court in a Delaware suburb. Six dead. Fourteen wounded. As the anchor man cut to a correspondent standing outside the mall, laughter rattled the bar. William swiveled his stool toward the sound. Framed by the front window, two couples sat at a table sharing a pitcher. One of the men, snapping peanut shells and tossing them into his mouth with a cocky precision that instantly made William despise him, sported a cowboy hat, and leaned back with his noodle legs resting out from under the table like he wanted to ensure everyone in the bar saw his new pointed toe westerns. The other one, less obviously concerned by fashion, wore a t-shirt and flannel, and squirreled a golf ball-sized wad of chew in his cheek that he'd spit into an empty soda can every now and then. In his state, William had a hard time distinguishing the ladies. Both blondes were evidently unafraid of a hairspray can, and wore tight jeans and pumps.

He gawked at them—a mix of drunken wonder and disgust—longer than social mores considered polite, as one might regard a masturbating monkey at the zoo. Unaware William was staring at them, the couples talked in boisterous, mirthful tones. Just some friends having a nice night out. The clean-cut cowboy mumbled something and the entire table erupted in laughter that seemed unnerving in the quiet bar.

"Booorinnng! Booorinng!" William hollered over them.

Shaken from their world, the couples' heads snapped towards him, seeing William leaned forward in his stool, making no attempt at subtlety—a corner of his mouth crept in a semi-hostile smirk.

He shook a thumbs-up at them. They frowned back.

William spun his stool back to face the bar and sipped his drink. He yapped at the man on the countertop game a few times. The man only shrugged and stared at the screen. After awhile, Lewis noticed William's empty glass and set another in its place with a fresh napkin. William paid for the refill, then sea-legged to the

55

bathroom to piss.

When William returned, the two ladies from the table were at the juke, casually scrolling its catalog. Seeing them, he perked up, his neck jerking back in surprise, and staggered to them. He rested an elbow on the machine, stared into its glow, and grunted.

"Kenny Chesney?! No way. Dogshit. We're not listening to that." He gently inched between them and the touchscreen.

"What are you doin'?" one of them said.

William tapped at the screen. "Sorry. Ain't gonna happen. You're not gonna ruin everyone's night."

"Oh—my—fuckin'—gawd. What an asshole. Can you believe this?" she said to her friend. Over at the table, the men were engaged in their own conversation, but hearing their ladies' voices, they hopped up toward William.

"William—quit messin' around," Lewis said from behind the bar. "He's just messin' around. Likes to give people a hard time."

William swatted the air behind him like Lewis' words were mosquitoes. "Nah, Lewis. No. Fuck that shit. Black Sabbath."

"Well, I don't care if he is messin' around. He needs to quit before he get hurt." The men stepped between their ladies and William, hesitating a few feet from him. William stared at the screen.

"That's our money, we can play what we want," the blonde announced over clean-cut cowboy's shoulder.

"So what? This ain't a democracy." William pressed a button and Geezer's plodding bass intro to 'Children of the Grave' boomed over the bar.

56

"Yeah," the man at the countertop said.

"Right? Right?" William said and pointed to the man. "I knew I liked you for a reason."

"Isn't he that new cop?" the other blonde said.

"You're goddamn right I am," William turned from the screen, "and by order of the Black River Police Department I forbid you to touch that screen."

The two men strong-armed William from the juke.

"Get your hands off me. I'll haul you mouthbreathers in."

"For what, motherfucker?" The flannelled man said.

"Guys, come on—I'm sorry," Lewis said, rounding the bar. "William, time to go."

Lewis separated the men from William, pushing him toward the back exit before they could hit him. He threw his hip into the push bar and pivoted William outside. Then he hung an arm in the door jamb and said, "Dammit, William. You need to watch yerself. Quit actin' like a stupid shit—you're a goddamned officer of the law." He shook his head and sighed, let the door swing close.

William brushed off his lapels and stumbled away from the door into the empty parking lot. To his right, beyond a chain link fence, the dim glow of a street light hung in the side alley. He stood there for a moment and then, as if not knowing what else to do, lit a cigarette. He hadn't eaten since the Ballyhoo. Three puffs in his stomach turned and he felt the eggs were on their way back up. He hustled to the opposite end of the parking lot, threw his hands against the brick wall, let his head fall between them, and spit.

Nothing came up.

After waiting a moment, the sensation subsided. William wiped his mouth and, deciding to walk home, turned from the wall with a wild step directly into a fist.

The punch launched him to the concrete. He vaguely registered the two men from the bar as they descended on him, pummeling him with shots to the face and stomach. He definitely felt the tips of those new boots. William didn't fight back—he just let his head fall, laughing and spitting blood onto the sidewalk.

"Fuckin' freak," the flannelled man muttered before launching a chew loogie into William's face. Then the two men disappeared out of his line of vision.

On his back, William stared up into night, trying to focus on the stars, feeling the world rotate above and beneath him. As the queasiness returned to his stomach, he was struck by their loveless intensity—cold radiance of metal—felt their distance gnaw at something inside as if they were a half-forgotten memory. Something was building, not only within himself, but all around him. In everything. The world—drawing up on hind legs. His heart rose with it. A warm tingling passed through him. Out to his finger tips and toes. Back to his center. At his armpits, tight in his chest. He breathed heavy, thought he might pass out.

Then he threw up on himself.

William came to—cold tile against his cheek and the urge to vomit. Instinctively, he flopped from the bathroom floor to the toilet, clearing the rim as his stomach cast its contents into the water. He collapsed against the tub, eyes watering, and anticipated the next round. It never came. But he'd rather been dead. He couldn't remember ever feeling this bad and he promised it was the last time. Pressure clustered behind his eyes and cheekbones like ten thousand little men swinging sledgehammers against the inside of his skull. He kneaded his sinuses with his thumbs and rubbed the back of his neck.

At the sink, William inspected himself in the mirror. His face was tender and warm. Nostrils covered in dried blood. A welt circled his right eye. His bottom lip was split open, reminding him of a torn sausage casing. Parts of the previous evening returned to him, and he looked down at the dried puke on his shirt and tie, smelled the tangy bile of chewing tobacco. He sighed and doused warm water over his face until the blood was gone.

William heaped a teaspoon from a sachet of pharmaceutical grade salt into a neti pot on the sink. From the cupboard, he retrieved a jug of distilled water and poured it into the ceramic mug. Then he picked it up, tilted his head forward, and put the spout to one nostril. Water trickled out the other nostril into the sink basin. After blowing his nose into his palm, he repeated the process on the other side.

William sipped coffee and watched the sunrise from his kitchen window, hoping to kick start his mind out of slow motion. The shower hadn't helped. It still felt as though someone else operated the controls, certainly

59

he never got up from the bathroom floor. No way was he going anywhere today.

He'd call in sick.

He turned away from the window, zombie-shuffled to the kitchen table, and eased into a seat. Another sharp burn shot up his nostrils and he pushed the bone under his eyes again. Each heartbeat rang out in his brain like a gong. He snatched a prescription bottle of Adderall from the table and twisted off the cap. He held an orange gelatin capsule between his fingers and studied the small beads inside. All the XR beads were mixed with the IR beads—no distinguishing them.

Grabbing both ends of the pill, William rotated each half until it eased apart. He shifted the beads between the two capsule halves until both seemed to contain an even amount. But there was no way to know. Why bother? From his jacket pocket he drew a tissue and tore off two corners. He stuffed each half of the pill with a tissue piece, and then popped one into his mouth and washed it down with coffee. He placed the other half back in the bottle.

Standing up, he changed his mind and fished out the half from the bottle and dropped it into his pocket.

William hovered over the table, feeling like a spent shell casing on cold concrete. He rubbed at his face again. He forced himself to choke down the last of his coffee, and then located his keys, put on his sunglasses, and headed out the door.

Hands shoved into his flannel overcoat, Robert ventured across their backyard with Carson lagging five feet behind. At the end of the property, they hopped the low split rail and hiked up the small incline leading into the woods behind the house. It was Ernie Dodd's land officially, but it'd never been an issue in the ten years they'd been here.

"Generally, it's best to find a standing dead tree." Carson was looking down at his feet as he kicked leaves. "Carson, are you listening?"

"Yeah, dad." He stopped kicking. And then he squinted and asked, "How you know which ones are dead without the leaves on em?"

"The bark will be exfoliating off."

They continued on for several yards.

"What's that mean?"

"Peeling away from the tree."

They broke left and walked deeper into the thicket, a wave of red leaves parting at their feet. The air was crisp, and the sun was trying to break free from grey clouds. Fifteen feet ahead, a fox darted past their path. Carson had his head down again, playing in the goddamn leaves. Robert wanted to tell him to look, but the fox had gone.

"Carson, keep your eyes in front of you," Robert snapped.

"Okayyyy. You don't have to yell."

"Just pay attention."

Robert knew his son would rather be inside playing video games, but Carson was getting to the age where he needed to start learning how to be a man.

Armageddon was coming in some form or another and when the shit hit the fan, he'd need to know more than how to press 'x' or 'y'. Real world skills.

They walked on in quiet. Carson's jeans swished amid his stride, accompanied by rustling leaves and a nearby crow.

"Dad, there's one." Carson stopped and pointed.

Not far from them, a dead tree stood. It angled slightly to the left, broken off about five feet up. The rest of it lay on the ground.

Robert smiled a toothy grin that showed through his beard. "See what happens when you're paying attention?" He patted his son on the shoulder. "Good job."

A smile escaped Carson's reddened face.

When they reached the tree, Robert unsheathed the hatchet at his side, and chopped away a thick branch. "See, the core will be white, not green," Robert said, showing Carson. "You can probably just snap them off."

Carson broke a few small branches.

"First thing we need is a fire board and spindle." Robert split the thick branch in two, and cut off the bark like it was unwanted crust on a slice of bread. He fashioned the half into a modest plank and, satisfied, set it next to the tree. Then he cut a long branch from the fallen half of the tree, and broke it down until he had a straight eighteen inch stick. "Here, clean the knots off this."

He handed the stick to Carson, who took his knife from his coat.

"Remember to cut away from you."

"I know."

While his son was busy with the stick, Robert used his foot to sweep away a large circle in the sea of leaves. Once Carson had finished the spindle, the two went about collecting more kindling, processing the wood into four piles according to size and width.

Taking his own knife from the inside pocket of his flannel, Robert notched one end of the plank. "Once you have this, then you make a divot for the fire hole." He tucked a leaf under the small opening. "See, this way our cherry will fall down and collect on this leaf here."

He knelt down on one knee, and braced the plank under his other boot. "You wanna position yourself like this. Like yer a knight kneeling before a king. Here, lemme see that." Robert grabbed the spindle from his son. "You're still too little for this part, but just watch." He set the bottom of the spindle into the divot, and balanced it between his hands. "Rub em together like you do when you're cold." He quickly massaged his palms together, the spindle revolving between palms and pointer fingers. After a few seconds, Robert continued his motion down the spindle, and, reaching the bottom, started from the top again.

He repeated this process a half dozen times. Soon a thin wisp of smoke trailed up from the divot. Increasing speed, he made two more passes, and then dropped the stick to one side. A quarter-sized cherry bloomed from the leaf.

"This will stay good for a solid five minutes," he said, carefully raising the leaf. "Here, hand me that." He pointed to the tinder bundle next to Carson. Carson complied and Robert dropped the smoking cherry into the bundle. "You can help with this. Come 'ere." The boy joined his father, slight hesitation on his face. "Just blow."

Together, the two blew into the bundle. In no time, gusts of smoke poured from the tinder, and the cherry amplified into a flame. Before his fingers could be burned, Robert tossed the bundle onto their dirt circle.

"Easy peasy."

They slowly fed the small flame, gathering handfuls of wood from the outer rim of their circle.

"I wish we woulda brought marshmallows," Carson said. His eyes glimmered as he gazed into the fire.

Robert grinned, pulled a 10 oz. bag of Jet-Puffed Giant Roasters from his flannel, and chucked it to Carson.

8

The car kicked up a crawling swell of dust as William steered down the dirt road to the Wolfe property. The headlights illuminated a scrap of weathered split rail. Left of the road, Hoyt Steven's cornfield had depleted to a bleary ecru. William parked at the end of the drive and looked out at the modest farmhouse. Amber light emanated from the front windows. The old Gambrel barn hung back seventy yards, among knotted weeds and dying grass. Beyond it, bright stars silhouetted a large copse.

He let himself in the back door—Lionel kept it unlocked—and ascended the small foyer stairs to the kitchen. The house—filled with his father's restored furniture and his mother's books—was silent, warm light playing with shadows. Though he'd known no other childhood home, the rooms were foreign and distant now, containing only a faint dream familiarity. In truth, he felt out of place here.

William entered the living room to find Lionel slumped in a recliner, reading a folded newspaper. He smiled and got up to hug William, who accepted the embrace with a kind of semi-affectionate formality. The hesitation only increased the enthusiasm of his father's embrace. Lionel had spent forty years restoring furniture, the last twenty salvaging turn of the century wood from condemned buildings and homes around the region, and the work kept him in better shape than a man half his age. Or, at least, that's what he liked to say his doctor said. William had never met anyone who enjoyed their work more than his father. Lionel would be up and in his workshop before the first crack of sunlight. In the days before Sara got sick, it wasn't unusual for him to work twelve hours without a break.

"William—how are you?" Lionel asked.

"Fine. More importantly, how are you?"

Lately, William had been making excuses—mostly to himself—for not visiting more often. His father wasn't the kind of man to speak up when he needed help. Nor was he the kind to lob guilt onto his son.

"Good. She's been pretty coherent the last two days. We went for a walk this afternoon. It was nice to get outta the house—" Lionel paused and furrowed his brow, "Why are you wearing sunglasses this time of night, son?"

Shit. William hadn't taken them off since leaving the station. He instantly regretted the visit. Should have stayed clear until the bruising went down.

Lionel pulled the glasses away. "What the hell happened to your face?"

"Outside light burned out. I tripped over the bushes taking the garbage out. Looks a lot worse than it is."

"I'd say—looks like you were in a brawl and you got your ass handed to you."

William chuckled. "That's what everyone at the station said, too." Everyone except Sheriff Fry had

66

accepted his story about the light and the bushes. When he came around for an update on the Grass murders, Hollis examined William a long while—the kind of look that said he wasn't buying it—and finally shook his head in frustration. He seemed too exasperated to even comment, only pulled up the back of his pants and lumbered away.

"Fittin' into things all right?" Lionel asked him this question every time he visited. If fitting into things meant burning fresh tweak holes into his brain and living on a diet of nicotine and whiskey, then, yeah—he was fitting in *just* fine.

William shrugged.

"Like I said before you moved back—I can't even stand a trip to the Piggly Wiggly. If I had the choice, I'd rather not go at all. Everything's boarded up or well on its way to being."

William's mind slipped back to the night before, lying on the parking lot, sharp rocks poking into his skin, staring up at the cold moon. With all the speed and aspirin he'd ingested throughout the day, the pain virtually disappeared. He even forgot about it in the latter half of the day. But standing there now, the memory jostled the aches back to the forefront of his consciousness. Inevitably, his shame tumbled along, too. You couldn't have one without the other.

He gnashed his teeth. Tried to swallow it all, like a fourth shot of Wild Turkey on an empty stomach. He adjusted his shirt, cold sweats in his armpits and lower back, and propped himself against the door jamb. He pulled at his collar, clammy sweat there.

"And what about Sheriff? Gettin' on with him?"

Lionel's question jogged William back to the living room. "I can tell you I like it better when he's not around."

Lionel laughed. William massaged his jaw with his thumb and index finger.

"Yeah, Hollis can be an ass sometimes, but he's not a bad man." Lionel looked to his left as if there was a question written on the wall. William followed his gaze. "You know, back in school, he used to have the hots for your mom," he said with a smirk.

William laughed. The sound seemed inappropriate inside the house. "No shit?"

"Then again, who didn't?" Lionel said to himself. "Can't blame him. Poor guy never stood a chance against my wiles." Lionel mocked an old one-two toward William's shoulder.

"Oh, really?" William threw up his palms, pretending to block the shots. "So that's how you won mom's heart. You conned her. Great—good to know, Lionel." Lionel had always referred to his father as Albert. As a child, William thought it was strange and finally asked him the reason. Lionel said once he turned eighteen Albert was just another man. The next day, much to Lionel's chagrin, William began calling his father by his first name.

He was ten.

"No—it was love at first sight," Lionel said, dropping into a serious tone. "Knew from the jump she was the girl I was gonna marry. Nothin' woulda kept me from her. Not Hollis Fry. Not a goddamn movin' train."

"Lucky she felt the same," William added without jest.

"Lucky for you." His words were light, but Lionel's smile faded. Blankness washed over him. His eyes watered.

A part of William, one that'd never admit it aloud, measured all men against Lionel's shadow. And it was a monolithic shadow, casting out far enough to engulf William, too. William didn't mind that so much anymore. In fact, he'd become thankful for it. But here in the living room, the warm light seemed to lay bare Lionel's infamous stoicism. He saw his father as he was. The wrinkles in his father's face were deep canyons in his arid skin, eroded over the course of seventy years by some barbarous river. William hadn't noticed the impossible until then: Lionel had gotten old.

William placed a hand on his father's shoulder. He needed a goddamn drink.

It'd been two years since Lionel and Sara shared a room. She slept in the old guest bed next to the bathroom on the first floor. Lionel had moved her there when her condition was just beginning to worsen. He didn't want to frighten her if she woke and didn't remember him. William recalled the night, a few months before he moved back, when Lionel phoned to tell him he'd been jolted from their upstairs bed by her screams. He had rushed downstairs, searching the darkened house until he found her by the backdoor. Curled up on the linoleum, she clutched a broken ankle, not knowing where or what she was. Since the accident, Lionel stayed on the living room couch, a few feet from her door.

William hunched forward in a rocking chair next

to Sara's bed, watching her while he sipped whiskey. Wisps of gray highlighted her dark brown hair. Her beauty had made her an exotic curiosity in a time when Basantes was the only Mexican surname in the county, and she looked as beautiful now as she always had. But her good looks could never surpass her intelligence and moral backbone. Both had made her an indomitable force within the community, and after retiring from her middle school teaching position, she held two consecutive four year terms on City Council. Despite fearlessness in the face of conflict, she maintained a kind and compassionate center toward everyone. Even her political opponents had a hard time finding a bad word against her.

William remembered her veracious appetite for life most—especially nurturing her own inner life—and her realm of interests was wide and varied. She always had a book in hand, learning something new. At the time it annoyed the hell out him, but William had not been absolved from his mother's obsessions. No doubt he was the only detective in Iowa to have a mother require self-study in the humanities. It was a gift, he realized now, Sara demanding more from him. This was most likely responsible for his eagerness to get the hell out of Black River after high school and never come back. She exposed him to the rest of the world, instilled a healthy discontent within him that drove him to look beyond the miserable easy and limits of Black River. If anything, Sara was at heart a passionate evangelical. Not one for dogma or church-planting, but one for self-improvement. She preached the sermon that you could be anything in this life with sacrifice and work. William believed her.

For a time.

He reached for her hand. Gently stroked it with his thumb. Kissed it. For a moment, wished he'd been a better son. But what did it matter now? He was a shell just as she was a shell. No longer the boy she once loved. No longer his mother.

William remained at the edge of the bed for a long time, sitting with her in silence.

9

Leon Hutchins rolled onto his back and tossed the silk sheet to the side. The sex was good, as always, but did little to ease his building inner tension. On the other side of the bed, Esmeralda took a drag off her cigarette, leaving red lipstick on the white filter, and eased the smoke out of her mouth, slowly inhaling it up into her nostrils, her dark brown hair unfurled to an exposed shoulder. But even here, under postcoital sedation, Leon recognized the brutality connected to her eroticism. No disentangling one from the other. Both a part of her since the beginning—Old Testament Lord with T&A. Bloodletting and Flesh. Just like those black and white circles the Chinese were so fond of.

As he tried to catch his breath, lungs feeling like dried prunes, it occurred to him in some far off region of his brain that he may have taken a wrong turn some ways back. The odd sensation had gnawed at him since the night before, and he tried to shove it back into whatever mental drawer from which it sprung, but it proved too elusive. It was like something was descending upon him, stalking him from above like an owl on a mouse, making him feel small and powerless.

Sitting up in Esmeralda's bed, he decided to attribute the weirdness to a lack of sleep. It'd been six, maybe seven, days. The heebie-jeebies were hoppin' out of everything, starting to turn his thoughts to mush. Definitely due for a little beddy-bye.

Leon stared at his Queen, and again tried to push away the sensation.

Their history went back five years to when he ran small change for a low-level dealer and pimp in Hegemony named Quadell Lenz. Leon and Quadell, a pair of snake eyes in an alley game of Craps, tumbled into each other's lives when they both landed in a residential behavioral management program at fifteen. They discovered a mutual love for bedlam and vehemence toward the world, and the two quickly became the ebony and ivory of New Choices Treatment Center. The music they created together, a kind of Ornette Coleman approach to violence, lead to several riots, fires, beatings, countless stays in isolated containment, and an attempted rape of the facility's nurse. The institution finally separated the two six months after meeting when Leon stabbed a residential counselor in the eye with a pencil and was relocated to a psych ward in southern Iowa.

Years passed. Leon drifted out of Iowa into the outskirts of American life like a smokestack puff of chlorofluorocarbon. Quadell stayed in Hegemony, slowly graduating from petty crime to local underworld factotum, inevitably steering himself into an Iowa Correctional Facility jumpsuit. During his five year incarceration, Q, as he was known, did not find Jesus or Mohammad. Taking up the pen, he found another savior, and soon saw himself as a direct literary descendant of Iceberg Slim and set sights on a new hustle.

After his release, Q returned to Hegemony, with a

two hundred page manuscript called *The Ice Fiend*, and another untitled half-completed follow-up. With a new direction, but needing cash, he wasted no time returning to his old life, while he secured an agent in New York, and waited for publishers to come knocking.

It was during this time, Leon hooked back up with him.

He met Esmeralda one night at Q's squalid one bedroom above Fourth St. Pawn and Gun. She was one of his girls graduated to main squeeze. Q, fisting a bottle of Olde English, had cracked the apartment door, revealing her fanned out on the couch like a thrift store Cleopatra. Leon strolled into the room without waiting for an introduction, kissed her hand and said, "Well, aren't you a queen." He had dropped in to pick up some product, but Q invited him to stay and the three drank, trying to forget the thick July air, a beat up fan in the window, drowning out the street life jangle below. Q and Leon recalled stories from their youth. Esmeralda listened in silence, forearm and lazy wrist poised over the arm of the couch. But as night gave way to dawn, another forty freshly drained, Q misinterpreted her calm as icy conceit, and split her lip. She ended up needing stitches. Even years later, the hairline crack was still visible. In Leon's estimation, it merely added to her allure.

Several months rolled by before Leon ran into her again. He had stopped by to speak with Q. She answered the door, sporting a purple ring around her right eye (she made that shit sexy though), said Q had been MIA for a week. Back then she hadn't tweaked, and after letting him in, Leon convinced her to cut lines together. He would later go on to see himself as the prime influence on what

74

was to come. In hindsight, Esmeralda was probably just pissed at Q. "Wow," she said, bobbing up from the coffee table and rubbing her nose, "That's better than any man I've ever been with." The comment made Leon's balls seize up and something in his heart wither, but soon, she was straddling him with her tongue in his mouth and unbuttoning his shirt.

Unsurprisingly, Esmeralda quickly developed an insatiable appetite for tweak and, in the following weeks, called Leon more and more. What *did* surprise Leon was her curiosity about the whole shebang. Most birds just wanted to know how much he was holding, what they could do to get that right price, but she frequently inquired about sales, quantities, dealers and distributors.

One night at the Cellar King, the two had emptied a bottle of bottom self scotch, slow dancing to Nina Simone's version of "Strange Fruit" and playing a sloppy round of grab ass in the back corner by the juke. Leon knew something had been nibbling her attention since he picked her up. That being so, what she finally proclaimed when they returned to the bar still floored him. "We break away from Q and go out on our own, bypass his guy directly to the regional distributor." Her voice was authoritative, suddenly sober, as if she hadn't been drinking at all.

Leon howled and slapped the bar. "Must be hammered. Q just gonna let usss fuck im over? He's rattled your brain one too many."

Esmeralda's face turned serious. Leon would come to know the look well. It was one that preceded bloodshed.

"Come on, now. And where we find enough

money to convince this honcho we're major league?" He turned away from her to check his look in the mirror behind the bar, taking a slow pull from his glass. "I admire the moxy, but you haven't sold a teener."

"Q has forty five thousand stashed in the ceiling hatch of his place." Her eyes hadn't left him, hadn't lost any of their hypnotic aggression.

Leon's droopy eyes widened a little. "Mmm . . . and what about Q?"

"Just see about a meet and greet."

"'N what makes you think thisss honcho's gonna even agree to that?"

"I shoulda known. Shoulda went ahead and done this myself. You're too much of a pussy," Esmeralda sighed.

Leon snapped back his head with a wicked smile, finishing his drink, slammed the empty glass down and danced his fingers up past the hem of her mini. "Let's not get it twisted now, Queenie."

Two nights gone in a meth-blink, and Leon was ascending the rickety pull-down latter to the small unfinished attic in Q's place. Dark and cobwebbed, Leon felt around blindly until he pulled down an unwashed pillow case full of cash. He counted it at the kitchen counter, while Esmeralda buried a hand down his pants.

Minutes later, Q tumbled through the door, drunk and spaced, and about shit his pants when he laid eyes on his rainy day fund spread over the counter and his lady giving Leon head.

Leon managed a sheepish smile—his erection went limp at the click of the lock—and muttered, "Q . . . I know this probably ends our friendship but I just wanna say—"

Q stormed forward with gnashed teeth, face balled up like a fist, and groaned, "You bitches! I'm gonna fuckin' kill both you!"

Leon reached his .44 Magnum and fired as Q crossed the living room. It tore a chunk from his shoulder, but the behemoth lurched on and landed a running right hook that sent Leon staggering to the floor, pants to his knees, cock flopping about like a flag on a windy day. Q plummeted down and continued to punish him with shots to the face. Leon was on verge of losing consciousness when Esmeralda drove a ten inch chef's knife into Q's back. He whipped around with a blind backhand but missed. She came down with another blow to his back. He fell into the wall and she knifed him in the stomach repeatedly until his strength left him and he slid all the way down. Then she was on top of him, sending the knife into him again and again. Blood oozed out of him in every direction and when his eyes finally went lifeless, Esmeralda continued to stab him. Leon had to pull her off, saying "I think you got im, love."

They rolled the body inside the living room rug and ditched it in an alley four blocks away. Two days later the police discovered Quadell Lenz with thirty-seven stab wounds, his cock severed and stuffed in his mouth. They suspected a gang-related hit but the investigation quickly went cold.

Things moved fast after the slaying. Esmeralda wooed the distributor and within six months she'd purged or amalgamated the region of all opposition and cornered the market on the Midwest meth trade. By the next year, she was dealing directly with California.

"Want another?" Esmeralda asked, sitting up in bed.

"Sure—why not?"

After snorting a line, and setting the mirror on the night stand, Leon sprung from the bed and wormed into his pants, while, simultaneously, hunting the room for his Chelsea boots. He found one as his phone rang.

"Oh, for fuck sakes," Leon hissed after seeing it was Big Deal.

"Problems?" Esmeralda asked.

"Just personnel." Leon sighed and answered the call. "Hey fuckface, why are you callin' me? You tryin' to fuck me?"

"Shit man—Leon, I'm sorry but you gotta cycle back to BR. Like, pronto, yo. Shit hit the fan—Georgie Boy and Frankie—"

"Whoa, whoa—ease up on the gas, son." Leon located his other boot and sat back on the bed. He jerked one on with both hands, squeezing a heel into it.

"Georgie Boy and Frank got dropped."

Leon's eyebrow shot up. "Whaddya mean?"

"We was at Frank's and some buster came in—wasted Georgie Boy. Point blank, man. Point. Blank. Then he took out Frank."

"Why you just gettin' to me now?"

"Man, dude, been tryin' to get at you forever. That's what I been tellin' you, yo. You don't check yer voicemail?"

Leon surveyed the room. "Uh . . . I been busy with things."

"Leon, I'm scared. I was there. Dude seen me and tried to sleep me."

"What he look like?"

"Grizzly white dude. Nazi inked. Dude is crazy, man—I'm tellin' you."

"Listen, I'll be back in a bit. Change your diaper and sit tight."

Leon killed the call and put on his other boot.

"Georgie Boy and Frank are dead."

Esmeralda jerked forward. "What?! What's going on down there? You sure you got this under control?"

Leon sighed. "This ain't my first rodeo. Your lack of faith breaks my heart, love." He buttoned his shirt, wiggled into his suit coat, and then into his leather.

"Just be sure you do." She gave him the look.

All pistons running now, Leon broke from the room like he was late for a bus.

Leon gunned his '68 Charger down a dark back road ten miles from Esmeralda's compound, tree branches smacking the windshield. He barely rolled to a stop in front of the forest-veiled barn before throwing it into park and leaping out. Two Mexicans, whose names he hadn't bothered to remember, wielded assault rifles his way as he approached the barn doors.

"Hey, now . . . it's me," he said, scratching impatiently at his horseshoe mustache.

They nodded and relaxed their rifles.

"Come on now—lemme in. Apúrate!"

One of the men ushered him inside, through the dark interior still stinking of horse, and into a back stall. The man picked up a push broom and swept the hay to one side. Then he and Leon pulled up part of the flooring. There a set of stairs lead to a metal door.

Leon fiddled with a string around his neck, pulling up a key attached to it. Without taking it off, he unlocked the door and flipped the light switch to the 8x8 concrete room. Against the walls, boxes of cell phones, ammo, scales, and a large amount of cash filled steel shelves. A cache of guns leaned upright in the corner like broomsticks. Toward the back was a folding table covered by a tarp. The Mexican threw back the tarp and eyed Leon.

"This the new shit?" Leon asked.

"Sí. Cuanto?"

Leon hesitated. The gears turned inside his head. Queenie would get over it. "Cuanto?! Fuggin' all of it, ese. Let's go—pronto." He slapped his hands together.

The man yanked two duffle bags from a nearby hook.

Leon, AK slung over his shoulder, heaved the duffle bags into the Charger's trunk. Then behind the wheel, he fired up the engine and peeled back toward the highway.

Twenty minutes later, the Charger careened south on Route 13 to Black River, Howlin' Wolf's "Spoonful" spewing from the window, and Leon's glassy eyes fluttering in his cranium like fireflies in a jar.

10

Roland tugged at his hoodie strings, and shouldered the Rock Bottom's filthy glass door, bushwhacked by an REO Speedwagon tune as he entered. The place was crowded and brimming with volume and heat and he zigzagged unnoticed between the boisterous patrons, peanut shells crunching under his boots as he reached the bar and secured the last stool near the exit. Delilah was busy at the other end, but spotted him sit, and after serving two pints from the tap came over, wiping her hands on a towel tucked in her back pocket.

"Usual, honey?" she said. She flashed a smileful of meth-rot—souvenirs from her and Ray's time down the tweak mine.

He nodded, resting his arms across his legs, sleeve ends balled up inside his palms. She hurried down to the cooler.

Next to him Old Man Henry watched baseball on the TV behind the bar. Roland hadn't seen him for years. Assumed he was dead. Old Man Henry was one of a handful of black folk in town. He'd worked as a knocker on the kill floor in IMP's heyday. The knocker was the only employee to ever see cattle both sentient and insensible. The way Roland heard it, he went about the task with unusual enthusiasm. Maybe just bullshit, but due to the nefarious distinction, the knocker bore a messianic weight—a cross made of cow brains—for the rest of the plant who psychologically distanced themselves of any responsibility. On average, Old Man Henry shot a captive bolt gun into 2,500 cows' brains a day, one every twelve seconds. 365 days a year for thirty years. Roland couldn't calculate that kind of math in his head, but decided to figure it out when he got home.

"That's it, Jimmy," Old Man Henry said to the TV, clapping loudly. "Two more now. Two more."

Delilah returned and placed a PBR and a shot of Jameson in front of Roland.

"What's the—how much do I owe you?"

"On the house."

"Well, I apprec—thank you, Dee."

She patted his hand. "No problem, honey. How you doin'?"

"Better now."

"You need to move on from her. It's been a long time. The two of you were never any good for each other anyway. Toxic. You know that."

Roland didn't respond.

"Je-sus Christ. How can that not be a strike?! That's gotta be a strike. You gotta give Jimmy a strike on that one," Old Man Henry barked at the TV.

"Henry—you need another?" Delilah asked.

"Yep," he said without looking away from the game. "Take the pitch. Take the pitch, Jimmy. . . Goddammit. For god's sakes . . . that was after the strike.

After the strike. How you call—oh, geez—squirrel was on the field after the Goddamn pitch! That's how they're gonna do it then. Probably stowed that little fucker in their bags to let loose. That's what you gotta do if you gonna do it then . . . for god's sakes."

Delilah poured a beer from the tap and came back and set it down for Henry.

"Still a buck quarter, right? All night it should be the same."

"Dollar seventy five. Has been for years, Henry."

"Well, jus make sure it stay the same all night when you put it down on my tab there."

"I'm not gonna overcharge you. Come on now."

"Well, okay—just sayin'—all night it should be the same. You know what I mean? None of that funny stuff."

"Henry—"

"I'm just sayin'—should stay the same now. Cheapest prices in town but still . . . ." Henry trailed off, lured back to his game by some play on the field.

Roland finished his beer.

"Knockin' em back tonight?" Delilah moved to grab another can.

"Gotta be good for something," he mumbled to himself. Roland slammed his shot and, as he did, his hood fell back. Old Man Henry noticed him for the first time.

In the old days Roland and Rosemary drank here most nights, caroused with regulars like Old Man Henry now and then, buying drinks as if dollar bills were lint from his pockets. There was never a shortage of neon friends, who always burned brighter the later it got— backslapping best pals, spewing confessions and regrets and dreams. But the neon inevitably went out with every bar close and rising sun, sharing no more than a nod the next night on the way to a stool.

"Holy hell, boy—what you 'posed to be?"

Apparently, that light had been out far too long for Old Man Henry.

Roland flipped the hood back over his head. "Never you—why don't you just watch your—go back to your game—Hen—old timer."

"When I was a boy, we use to pay a dime to see somethin' like you."

"That's enough, Henry. I'm gonna cut you off," Delilah said, returning with Roland's beer.

"What—I didn't mean nothin' by it. Boy looks off is all. Talks weird, too. Like the words is all jumbled up comin' out the mouth."

She put the beer down next to Roland's crumpled dollar bill and change. He pounded the beer, some leaking from the corner of his scarred mouth, and then stood up, tugging again at his hoodie strings.

"Oh—that's right—you the guy. The one blew hisself up in that fire. I 'member now," Henry added.

"Don't go, Roland. He didn't mean it. He's not right in the head."

"Nah, it's cool. I know."

"What you mean I'm not right in the head?"

"Oh, shut up, Henry."

Roland turned, stuffing both hands into his hoodie pockets, and shambled out the back like he'd never been there. On the dark walk to his mother's home, joints aching again, his mind circled memories of Rosemary and loss. When he reached the basement he got out a pencil and an old disability check stub. He pushed aside a few DVD's and, with his sleeve, wiped the cigarette ash from the glass of the coffee table. Holding the pencil like a child fists a crayon, he calculated the numbers. Old Man Henry's final count was roughly 27,375,000 cow's brains.

Roland wondered if any calculable total existed for his own life.

11

The sun had only broke the distant hills but Miguel could already feel its warmth bleed into the darkness under Black River Bridge. He opened his eyes. The water chopped sedately at mud and weeds and rock where debris collected in small pockets along the shore. An empty Big Slurp bobbed against a splintered plank a few feet from his blanket. Next to him, the small fire was nothing but ash. He lay there for a minute without moving, head on his school bag, and almost slipped back to sleep.

Then he yawned, catching a whiff of his breath. He rolled his tongue over the roof of his mouth and the back of his teeth. The inside of his mouth felt as nasty as it smelled. He spit, trying to launch it out in a glorious arch, but it split in every direction and dissipated nowhere near the river. He wondered how men's saliva maintained viscosity and trajectory so well. He sat upright, his back stiff from the cold concrete, and wiped away pebbles embedded in his cheek.

He stood up, casually brushing dust and rubble from his jeans, and then he folded the damp comforter, laid it out on the ground, and rolled it up like a sleeping bag. He shoved it between the graffiti-filled wall and a set of good-sized stones. With school bag slung over his shoulders, Miguel ventured out from under the bridge on a muddy path overgrown with brown grass and beer cans.

He slipped a hand into his pocket and discovered a crumpled paper there. He pulled it out and smiled as he unraveled a ten dollar bill. After returning to Justin's house the night before, the three boys had stolen thirty bucks from the weirdo that came home with Justin's mom. Looking at the bill, Miguel realized he was hungry. He wasn't sure what time it was—the Ballyhoo didn't open until seven thirty and he couldn't trek all the way to that part of town and still make it to school on time. He'd settle for the gas station. Maybe Eugene would be working.

He took in the river as he walked, his sleepy thoughts dancing in his mind like the light upon the water. Dead fish decomposed somewhere close. He walked until the embankment dropped on his right. The soles of his shoes were worn down and the dew made climbing the levee impossible. He'd tried before. Ended up sitting in class all day with dirt coated jeans and scrapes on his elbows, the kids laughing at him. Last thing he wanted was to stick out. As the years went by, he preferred the opposite—he wanted to disappear from life, to walk among the world like a ghost. For the first time since the night before, he remembered the hooded man with the scarred face.

Miguel neared an area where the ridge leveled with the ground. From where he stood he could make out the metal sign of the gas station five blocks away. He was turning to step into the tall grass and make his way out onto Route 7 when he saw the garbage bag and stopped. It was black and bottom heavy and laid slack in rocks an inch beneath the water edge, dark ripples slapping at one side, and the excess of the bag flapping loosely in the wind with a delicate crinkle that made him think of plastic fire. People were always finding something of value by the river. One time Justin came across a hunting knife, the kind with teeth in the blade. It looked brand new, just a bit of rust on the handle. It even had a compass on the bottom you could unscrew and store things inside. Miguel had never been so lucky. He took a step forward and nudged it with his shoe. It didn't seem like trash.

At the gas station, Eugene was working, but both of them were too preoccupied with shaking off the remnants of sleep to exchange more than a hello and a clumsy smile. Miguel bought a Mountain Dew and two breakfast burritos from the countertop warmer next to the register. He tossed his backpack in a booth and slid in beside it and devoured the food. As he ate, egg and meat dropped onto the wrapper and he grabbed them with his dirty fingers and shoved the pieces into his mouth, burrito grease dribbling from his lips. When the food was gone he twisted open the soda, still swallowing the last of the food, and chugged half the bottle as he stared out the front window. The sun did nothing to brighten the pencil-shaded day. He looked back toward the river and wiped his hands on his jeans.

He washed his hands and face in the bathroom. Then, locking the door, he took off his shirt and ran a wet paper towel over his neck and underarms—what his mother called a Mexican shower. After he finished, he examined the hair beginning to sprout in his pits—the new changes in his body held an odd fascination—until another customer banged on the door. He stuffed the dirty shirt in the school bag, trading it for a clean one.

Outside the gas station doors, Miguel hovered near the trash bin, eyeing Eugene who was helping a customer at the register. The wall clock showed twenty minutes to eight, which meant he had a half hour until he needed to be in his homeroom seat. He checked to make sure no cars were at the pumps, and then quickly sifted through the ashtray above the trash bin, and pocketed two half-smoked cigarettes before dogtrotting back to the river.

Miguel stepped through the tall grass, much of it beige or a watered down piss color, and wandered to the river. Once there he paused and looked around and then took one of the cigarettes from his pocket and lit it with a Bic he'd stolen from home. He coughed several times, a violent cough that turned his stomach and made him lightheaded, and he thought he might lose the breakfast burritos. But the sensation passed and he continued on to the spot where the garbage bag had been. He knelt down, water seeping into his jeans, and pulled the bag from the river. It was heavier than he expected, and swayed as he held it above the water. He backed up a few steps to drier land, clutching the bag with a stiff arm out before him like it was a giant dirty diaper. Another bout of coughing overtook him then, and he lost his grip and dropped the bag, the contents flopping out onto the rocks.

He looked down, wiping his eyes, reality or his mind or his pulse or all of them eddying around him as he registered a foot with toenails painted a deep crimson. There were other parts he couldn't decipher, but he really didn't take the time to—it was all just pale flesh and blood and bone—and he gasped and flicked the cigarette into the river and whirled around, slipping on the rocks and scraping his right palm, and he instantly hopped to his feet again undaunted, and bolted back toward the gas station to Eugene, unable to distance himself from the indelible stench.

PART TWO

THE HUNGRY GHOSTS

12

The headache followed William into a sleep too shallow for dreams, greeted him when the phone rang. He opened his eyes and he snaked over the lip of the tub to belly crawl toward the bath rug, his wet shirt and boxers sticking to his body and dripping cold water onto the tile. He flipped open the phone and expelled a primordial growl that served as a hello.

Sheriff Fry's voice boomed through the tinny connection on the other end. William pulled the phone a good six inches from his ear. As the sheriff barked away, hardly acknowledging William had answered, the connection gave way to digital chime, and a harsh wind blew into the receiver, but William got the gist of what the fat man said: another homicide.

Black River Bridge.

He laid there, head cradled by his arms, nose buried in the machine washable 100% microfiber, and lapsed back into a half-slumber where he didn't have to think. Then after a few minutes he shot abruptly from the floor, tearing off the cap from an Excedrin bottle, and slammed six with a snort from the whiskey that rested on the sink. He stomped down the hall to the bedroom and rummaged the dirty clothes piles until settling on an outfit that was clean enough for one more go—slightly damp, but smelled better than he did.

In the kitchen, after losing two minutes to locate his jacket, he dumped a 1000mg Vitamin C supplement packet into a thermos full of ice water, slammed it, and immediately prepared another before pocketing two reserves. He nabbed the thermos from the counter, keys and sunglasses from the kitchen table, and lit the day's first cigarette on his way out the door.

Everything outside was filtered through a dismal gray lens.

At the car door, glancing at the transparent reflection in the window, something seized his heart and his insides plunged like a shaken snow globe into a mineshaft. He moaned, and dropped into a squat, supporting himself with a hand on the car to keep from falling over.

The baboons were back—a whole marching band there in full regalia, jumping on the bed with their rotten teeth, clamoring with maracas, horns, toms and cymbals.

Listen to them. Aren't the little bastards cute?

Always playin' the same cacophonous tune—a catchy number that made him want to retreat into the house, maybe turn off his phone, eat a palmful of sleeping pills to ensure he went down and stayed down for at least a day, and hide under the safety of his blankets with the doors locked.

He could do it. Call the sheriff. Tell him he was sick. Bad take-out the night before. Sara was worse. Lionel was counting on the prodigal son. Fry would understand.

He tried to laugh off the absurdity. How irrational—had he regressed to a hundred and eighty pound child? He gnashed his teeth, beat a fist against his chest, and swallowed hard as if he could force the sensations down, like the worm at the bottom of a tequila bottle. He punctuated the show of bravado with a curse. Then, using an unsteady hand, William wiped away sweat from his forehead, and rubbed at his eyes.

In his mind, a wounded animal, intestines unspooling onto the pavement from a gash in its gut, limped from a ditch into the headlights of oncoming traffic, the entire world there behind the wheel to bear witness. His cheeks went warm.

Pussy.

He leaned back on the driveway pavement. Pebbles dug into his palms. It felt as if a boa constrictor had suddenly coiled around his heart. The corners of his vision became hazy. He thought he might pass out.

He took several slow deep breaths, allowing his lungs to fill completely with every in-breath, and held the air there to a count of six before exhaling.

Then, as quickly as it came, the deluge stopped.

From his place on the ground, he heard what sounded like a crowd of thousands. The applause—far away, at first—rose in volume and clarity until it was all he could hear. He realized then that they were cheering for him, awaiting their performer to take the stage.

The show must go on.

William stood up, pulled from his cigarette—the crowd on their feet in the apex of anticipation—and swung open the driver's side door. He sat down, checking his mask in the rearview mirror, and slammed the door.

Silence.

He started the car and reversed out the drive.

He pulled off the highway onto the gravel shoulder and parked between a squad and the CSU van. Two more patrol cars were in front of the van, and sheriff had angled his Jeep half in the grass beyond the shoulder. William made his way toward the river, the wind blowing his tie about. He readjusted it a few times, but as gravel beneath his shoes turned to damp overgrowth, another gust hoisted the tie over his shoulder again and he let it be. Reaching the ridge, he ducked under the yellow police tape, and descended the small slope, tall grass and weeds leaving wet streaks on his pants as he went.

At the bottom of the slope, ten yards ahead, a blue tarp laid along a muddy path held down against the wind by four rocks at its corners. Colette Lee knelt with her back to him, white Tyvek suit over street clothes, snapping digital pictures of what lay before her.

Further down the path, almost halfway to the bridge, Christopher Boos had his bloodhound, Doyle, on a leash. The dog's head swiveled back and forth in the tall grass, tail wagging merrily. Out on the water, the helmsman of a dented utility boat, a man William didn't recognize, hollered something unintelligible to Sheriff Fry, who stood along the opposite riverbank. There, on the far side, Darwin Cash matched Boos' and Doyle's pace. Fry hollered something unintelligible back to the helmsman.

As he approached Colette, William saw five

garbage bags lined on the tarp. She heard him and turned.

"Nasty business," she said.

He looked down. Two arms lay in four severed pieces on the blue plastic. The forearms ended at the wrists, flesh savagely frayed like an old sweater that'd been through the wash too many times. At the other end of the tarp, a foot with crimson-painted toe nails.

"Jesus. Looks like they used a butter knife."

"Yeah, turned 'er into a jigsaw puzzle. No head or hands," she said.

"Who was the lucky one?"

"Some kid. Walkin' down here before school. Widy's got 'im over at the Pump N Dump."

She let the camera dangle from the strap, waddled to the next bag in line, and scratched her nose with the back of her hand before opening it.

William knelt down next to her. She held out a box of gloves. He took a pair and slapped them on. He examined the limbs, carefully rotating each with his fingers. They all had a bluish purple hue. On the inner left bicep, he discovered a tattoo—a contour line of a nobleman, grasping an orb in one hand, a staff in the other.

"You get this?" he asked, looking up from the tattoo.

"Of course," Colette answered with a smile.

"Email me a copy—wouldya?"

"Sure. What is it?"

The helmsman's voice cut him off before he could respond. Their heads whipped toward the river. A diver in a wetsuit surfaced from the water, tapping the boat's side. The helmsman shuffled over to aid the diver.

"Another one," Colette said, watching the two men wrestle a garbage bag over the lip of the boat.

William rummaged through several pockets until he found his saline solution. Two sprays up each nostril.

Cigarette smoke flooded from the windows as Leon Hutchins gunned the Charger into the turn, shredding the sparrows' morning song in an angry growl that reverberated down the residential street. He rumbled, jaw clenched, edged forward on the seat, nearly leaning on the steering wheel. Parked cars packed both sides of the street. Leon nearly missed the house, anxieties tumbling through his mind as they were, and he had to stomp on the brake when he tried to make the driveway, drifting the rear slightly, and almost ramming a Honda Civic. He grumbled again to himself, and reversed into Big Deal's drive.

Leon jumped from the car, AK strapped to his side, his Chelsea boot soles scraping the pavement. He opened the trunk and shouldered both duffle bags.

At the door, Leon located his bump key, eased it into the lock, and tapped it with the butt of the gun. He flashed on the lock's tumbler, imagined the cylinder pins jump up, the key sliding into place as he turned it slightly.

The lock clicked open.

He barreled through the living room, calling for Big Deal. No response. He made the rounds through the house. The place was empty. Coming back from the bedroom, he spotted the bathroom door, and rushed in.

Big Deal drew a pistol from the bathtub, where he had been squatting.

Leon cradled his AK. "Not even if I was twenty years younger, fuckface!"

"Yo, homie, you scared the shit out of us," Big Deal said, his brow relaxing.

"What are you doing in here?" Big Deal put his gun down. Leon followed suit. "Hiding? You *are* aren't you?"

The muscle around Big Deal's bloodshot eyes twitched. "Man, I been waiting on you forever. Said you'd be right up."

"Got caught up somewhere else. Get the fuck out the tub, wouldya?"

Leon pulled aside the curtain over the kitchen window.

"You know this buster kilt Georgie Boy and Frankie?" Big Deal asked.

Leon didn't answer. His eyes darted back and forth. No movement in the alley. He searched the sky. No black choppers.

"Somethin' got you spooked? You're makin' me nervous."

Leon released the blanket, set down the duffle bags, and unloaded a Ziploc of product onto the table.

"Cwww—shit, dawg." Big Deal's eyes widened.

"Stop talkin' like a god damn cartoon character." Leon's right hand trembled. "We need to cut this tonight, Vern. Let's move on it. Now."

"A'ight, man."

"I'm serious, motherfucker. Now. Not sure, but I think I'm being tailed."

99

"That *billy* from the bar?"

"No, not 'that *billy* from the bar,'" Leon whined in a nasally mock tone. "The Feds. Maybe. Black chopper was tailin' me on the way in last night."

"Oh, shit—wha?"

"Or White Lightnin's gone to my head."

"I dunno, Leon . . . maybe we should let things cool down a bit, you know—"

Leon scowled, his eyes fresh with purpose. "Aren't you a big time hustler now?" He pointed the gun toward the kid. "So let's swing that dick and sell some shit."

"I dunno. The Feds? That guy—"

Leon knocked him upside the head, drove him into the wall, and pushed the AK to his nose. "Either he comes to kill you or I will. I can always find someone who wants a job."

"A'ight, man. I was just playin'."

Leon let him go and strode to the hall. One thing, for sure—if he made it through the next two days, shorty would have to go. "Fuckin' pussy—I swear," he mumbled.

"You're leavin'?! Where you goin'?" Big Deal asked.

Leon sighed at the front door then turned back to the kid.

"Cut it alone. And if you steal from me, or you fumble this, I swear on your mama's dry ass sandpaper labia, I will cut out your heart and feed it to that ugly cunt you call a girlfriend while I fuck her with this gun."

100

William cut across the highway back to his car, sporadic rain hitting his jacket. He paused at the driver side door. Everyone at the scene had left. A few remnants of ripped police tape flapped in the wind. He lit a cigarette and got inside the car. He started the ignition, cracking the window, but let it sit in park.

His mind returned to the kid, Miguel Rivera. He didn't have much to add, mostly he was just freaked out. Who could blame him? William was just thankful the kid hadn't come across the last bag. A severed foot was bad enough. Regardless of how hard he pushed it away, the moment Colette pulled it from the plastic kept returning to the forefront of his thoughts. The girl's face, or what was left of it, would tattoo his memory.

William reached into his jacket pocket—the special left breast pocket—and retrieved the bindle there. He made a fist with his left hand, tight enough to dimple the fleshy part between his thumb and first finger. He tapped a bit of powder into the nook and quickly snorted it.

He sat in silence smoking for some time, and watched the rain build against the windshield until it obscured the world completely.

13

At nearly three in the afternoon, after Morris sat and purred on his chest for five minutes, Roland pushed back the comforter, eased himself up from the couch, and lit a cigarette from the pack on the coffee table. His skin felt tight and inflamed, the muscles in his neck and arms so tense it felt like his bones had been whacked by a baseball bat in his sleep, his entire physical being one giant acne nodule waiting to burst. He sat there, slouching forward on his knees in a sad parody of the Thinker, thoughts on nothing but the score. He had torched through the last of his shit the night before, after returning from the Rock Bottom.

Too late in the day to make rounds collecting cans. Besides, it'd be at least a couple days for his hot spots to replenish. No money until the disability check landed Friday. He knew this as he passed out the night before, of course. Just as he knew the sun would rise. But, still under meth's incantation, it was nothing more than an abstraction then. Sitting on the couch, a palpable terror quickly overtook his physical pain.

He exhaled the last drag, stamping out the butt on the mountain in the ashtray. Orange-spotted filters disappeared under a gray blossom, its rim an undulating glow. He watched the embers go out. Thick smoke snaked from the ashtray, filled the basement with a sharp scent that pulled at his sinuses. He stood over the coffee table, waved it away with a scarred hand.

When he stood up, adrenaline kicked him into the zone. The hardest working man in Black River was punching in for the day.

One long shot left.

Daniel Paul Bible lived two blocks from downtown in a decrepit Craftsman on Russell—a forty minute walk from his mother's house. The rain had stopped before he woke, but the brooding sky kept urgency in his step, and a wind blew constantly into his face, breath from his dark hood trailing over his shoulder like a dead man's scarf. Most of the trip he dropped his head to one side to protect his earless hole. Reaching Russell, Roland beelined from the corner across the black top up to Bible's porch. Leaves whirled over the wet grass in the front yard. With the back of his hand, he knocked on the screen door. He breathed deeply, felt his heart pump away—the walk only partially to blame.

Roland had known Bible since kindergarten. Even then the scnuvabitch had a mean streak. He reveled in doling out misery to everything he encountered in life. The kind of kid who never tired of titty twisters, snake bites, slapping lunch trays from your hands in the cafeteria, or making you look foolish in front of the girls. One day in the final weeks of sixth grade—they walked home from school together in those days—Bible found a kitten roaming an alley. He burnt its eyes out with a cigarette and crushed its skull with a tree branch. Roland still hated himself for not stopping him. He only stood there. When he finally did move, it was to run away, Bible's laughter and the cat's agony ringing from the alley.

Roland never walked with him again.

In high school, Bible mellowed some, having discovered weed and LSD. He took on an affected stoner's smile, proclaimed, "Yah, Doooode!" whenever possible, wore hemp necklaces with Fimo clay 'shrooms, spun Doors' records, and stared for hours at the stolen black light poster that hung from his bedroom wall. For awhile, it seemed, he became a kind of hero for high school wastiods in town. Whenever Roland saw him at a house party, Bible's lackeys sat wide-eyed and Indian style as he philosophized about drug powers, conspiracy theories, and revolution. But no matter how much peace and love Bible laurelled upon himself, Roland never forgot that day in the alley. That was the real Daniel Paul Bible. Roland half-expected to see him and his yes men on the six o' clock, Black River's very own Jim Jones.

He did a stint in the army after high school (Papa Bible was adamant no son of his would turn out a 'faggot hippy'), but he was dishonorably discharged within a year. Around town, word was he went AWOL with a fourteen-year-old girl in Louisiana. Returning home, the old Bible re-emerged. Youthful days of pot and pretense gone, he graduated to the big boy table. Roland couldn't hold that one against him, he was there too. Bible soon became more volatile than before. They'd rub elbows now and again, but Roland more or less kept his distance.

He tried to hit Bible up a year before. Been more

trouble than it was worth. Roland swore he'd never use him again. But Roland swore he'd never do a lot shit. Only a matter time before he did it again. Last night he'd gone to a bar packed with people. Today he'd score from Daniel Paul Bible. Tomorrow he'd go stand outside Los Portales. Stupid shit.

Roland waited another thirty seconds and then knocked again. Nobody. He opened the screen door, stepped up onto the porch. Above him, a dim bulb dangled at the end of an exposed cord. Bags of empty cans and bottles walled the far side. He had the passing notion to just steal them and leave. The floorboards whined under his boots as he went to the door. A TV blared from inside.

He knocked a third time. Hard.

The TV volume dropped and Roland heard the house groan as someone stomped toward the door. A hand parted the curtain. Bible peered out, his right brow shooting up in bewilderment. The sides of his hair were short enough for another go at boot camp, but abruptly flared into an unkempt and greasy brown top, and he sported a goatee that extended two inches from his chin. He swung open the door, and displayed an athletic build.

"The fuck you want?"

"I was—do you mind letting me—could I talk to you inside?"

"No." He stared at Roland.

"Come on, Bible."

"Don't come here. Ever. Far as you know, I don't do shit no more." He slammed the door.

Roland swore to himself and punched the air, his hood dropping to his shoulders. He had half a mind to kick open the door and ransack the house. As if turning away from the bad idea, he wheeled toward the screen door, swearing again, and flipped the hood back over his head.

Halfway down the porch steps, the house door opened behind him.

"You got two minutes."

Bible smacked on the corner of his lip, scratched his head, tilting it slightly to the left like a dog in wonder. "You can't just stop in. This ain't a all night mini-mart. You need to call first. Is that clear?" He said, leading Roland into the living room.

"Yeah, man." Roland looked away. "Sorry."

"What you need?"

"Thinkin', maybe, like—was wonderin' if you were holdin'? Maybe a ball?"

Bible shook his head, clicked his tongue off the roof of his mouth. "Course." He stared at Roland. "How you payin'?"

"My disability check drops in two days."

Bible stared at him. Bottomless pit eyes.

"Two days. You know I'm good for it."

"Ain't frontin' you shit, bitch. We passed that point long ago."

"Come on, man—"

Bible adjusted the toothpick nestled in his mouth. "Nah, nah, nah. You know this, Roland. You wouldn't abide it neither. Used to be King Shit of Fuck Mountain, but it's more like the king of shit now, huh?"

Roland sighed.

Bible crossed the room to the end table, opened the drawer, and cut two lines from a small baggie. He leaned in, thumb on one nostril, and vacuumed a line with the other. He came up for air sniffing and rubbing his nose.

"That's some fire." He stared at Roland again. "Just funnin' you, Roland. Go right ahead. Mi casa, su casa."

Roland hesitated.

Bible curled a brow, pointed with his open palm toward the table like an angry TV game show assistant in a grand prize showroom.

Roland went through the motions. Bible wasn't lying—the shit was fire. Zip-A-Dee-Doo-Dah. His muscle tension gave way some.

"We'll work it out," Bible said.

Roland felt relieved. Bible had his fun, but would help him out after all.

"O—okay—good—like I say—I mean, thanks—my check drops Friday."

Bible just stared. The gaze could peel paint from a wall.

"That's not gonna do."

"Whaddya mean?"

"I'm not running a soup kitchen. Come back when you got some scratch." Bible stepped forward, eyes still locked on Roland, and grabbed his arm. "But you really think you can wait that long? Two days . . . that's an awfully long time for someone like yourself."

"Come on, man. Help me out. I'm good on it. You know that. Why are you fuckin' with me?"

"Get on your knees."

107

Roland's cheeks flushed, sweat surfaced under his arms. He pulled away.

"Fuck you." Roland spit out the words. If they were bullets they'd have floored Bible, but in his current state he couldn't defend himself, and he was afraid.

"Seriously. Get on your knees."

Roland retreated into the kitchen, hands shaking uncontrollably. He leapt for the door. Bible seized his hoodie. Roland turned and pushed back. It had the effect of a ten-year-old pushing a pro wrestler. Bible slapped away Roland's arms, and threw a right cross that drove him into the door. On the rebound, Bible grabbed his throat and muscled him face first to the floor.

Then Bible was on top of him.

"You wanna fuck around?" Bible hollered as he landed a blow to the cheek, holding Roland tight between his thighs. He struck him on both sides of the face and the back of the head. A prickle surged from where Roland's ear used to be.

Bible leaned all his weight forward, gripping the back of Roland's neck, like a man doing a one arm push up. It took several seconds for Roland to realize he was unbuttoning his pants with his free hand. Roland thrashed about on the cold tile, trying to fling him from his back.

For whatever reason, Roland's mind cast him back three years. A brutal summer, even for Iowa, and the month's air hung so heavy, it sapped the motivation to do anything but sit and drink beer between showers. He couldn't stand anything that coated his skin, not even sweat, and during the summer Roland took five a day. The Occupants had recently returned from a month long tour, playing shit bars and house shows to tattooed young men—the 'rah rah boys,' as he called them—along the west coast, sleeping on couches or packed in with the gear in the van. They had to scrape together change to eat, but the time developing new material rejuvenated the band. He'd been up for two days driving, and after hitting town limits he went home and cooked.

By the night of the fire, August twentieth, the Shadow People had him held up in his trailer for six days. He'd encountered them before. Always in the peripheral. Eyeing him from behind the candy aisle while he waited in line at the gas station. Or sometimes they'd flash from a doorway or briefly appear in his rearview mirror. Whenever he snapped his head to get a better view, they'd be gone.

The encounters grew more frequent in the days leading up to the fire. Worse still, the Shadow People were becoming more brazen. It got to the point where he could feel their presence hovering outside his trailer in early morning hours.

Then they moved into the house. He'd enter the kitchen to get another beer or stroll to the bathroom to piss, and in the split second after flipping the light, he'd glimpse them scatter to the shadows like cockroaches. Their pitch black skin glistened like slippery orca flesh accented by patches of reptilian scutes. Bald featureless heads harbored white irises void of anything resembling humanity.

He'd gone to Milde's and bought a five pound bucket of nails, a hammer (he wasn't a handy man), a spool of monofilament fishing line, and an air horn. Then he drove out to Cedar Lake Road, loaded the van with

109

fence posts and whatever scrap wood he could scavenge from an abandoned farm. Roland went home and buried the air horn ten feet from his front door, leaving its red cone and button exposed. Using a six inch stick, he propped a flat granite slab over the horn, then covered it all in tall grass. He tied the monofilament to the stick, and ran a circuit around the trailer, and secured the line to an old tent stake. When he finished, Roland unloaded the salvage into the house and spent the rest of the night nailing it over the windows.

Bible slammed his head into the floor. A stream of blood poured from Roland's nose, Lucky Charms crumbs stuck to his cheek.

"That's it you ugly fuck. Gimme that shit," Bible shouted from behind him.

Roland screamed.

Close to five in the morning, the air horn went off. Roland shot from the couch, tossing aside his Strat, and looked out into the yard through a crack between boards. Nothing there. He soldiered to the back bedroom and peered out the barricaded windows. Only motionless night. Convinced the Shadow People were hiding in the darkness, he made the rounds of the trailer, stopping at every window to see if he could spot any incursion. In the meantime, feedback from the electric guitar left on the couch built into a shrill drone. Roland returned to the bedroom and rummaged his shotgun from the closet. Sticking a fistful of shells into his jeans, he peered out the living room window one more time, and then threw open his door, firing into the black of night. The sound cracked the silence.

He jumped the trailer steps and shuffled counterclockwise around the home. Under the trees behind the trailer, the Shadow People spoke to him for the first time.

Rooollie. Roooolannnnd.

The voices spoke in harmony, sounding like a kind of demonic barbershop quartet filtered through a Phaser pedal. He almost shit his pants.

In conjunction with the Black River constables, we have been watching you. You've upset the status quo, and they are coming for their pound of flesh. Escape is futile now. They'll hang you from hooks and make you suffer.

He reloaded and fired into the dark. Then he reloaded and fired again. Lights in neighboring trailers shot on. Dogs barked. Roland panicked and ran back inside. He paced the house, cursing, squinting out windows, and chewing his nails. On one lap, forgetting he set another alarm in the kitchen door jamb, his heel clipped the monofilament trip wire, and he fell to the floor, bottles clanging around him. He swore as he got to his feet. It was then that he heard the sirens.

He immediately stormed down the hall, leaped with flailing arms like he was grinding a rail, and landed on the raggedy accent rug outside the bathroom door. It slipped under the force of his foot, and he came down hard on his left side, his elbow and hip taking the brunt of the fall. Without processing the pain, he whipped into the door on all fours and flopped to the tub.

They are coming for you, Roland. They'll hang you from hooks and make you suffer.

In his frenzy, he tore back the shower curtain from the rail and reached into the tub where he stored his chemistry set. He gathered the empty flasks, glass cookware, rubber tubing, and Duracell packets, loaded

111

them into a cardboard box, hopped up from his knees, and ran to the hallway door. He kneed it open, the handle tolled against the exterior siding, and he heaved the box out into the yard, glass shattering as it landed somewhere in the dark. Then he was back at the tub, pouring everything down the drain—all the kerosene, paint thinner, denatured alcohol, brake cleaner, acetone, and anhydrous ammonia. Again on his knees, he slid to the sink cabinet, knocking over the box fan, grabbed a five gallon jug of hydrochloric acid and hauled it to the tub. As he dumped it into the drain, its vapor tore at his lungs and eyes. Finished, he pushed back from the lip of the tub and settled on the toilet, out of breath.

Out in the living room, the guitar's feedback eclipsed common sense, and, without thinking, he drew the Marlboros from his pocket and lit a cigarette.

Stupid shit.

The drain seemed to draw a deep wheezy breath and then exhale violently. An explosion blew out the bathroom window, the fence posts nailed there burned now like logs at a bonfire, the ceiling and walls engulfed by thick tongues of flame. It took less than a second, and Roland remained on the toilet seat for a moment, too punch-drunk to react.

He glanced down. The top of his shoes were gone, his shirt and jeans singed to tatters. He noticed then that the skin on his arms bubbled. He was cooking alive.

Outside the bathroom, the hall was on fire too, spreading out in every direction, and blocked his exit out the side door. He charged through the hall, the burning unbearable, and brushed at his left arm with the back of his hand. The skin there slackened, and dripped from him

112

like porridge from a spoon.

The flames hadn't yet reached the living room. Guitar feedback pealed in his head as he crossed the room to the front door. His fingers were melting, when he turned the gold-plated knob and pulled his hand away, some of the skin stayed there and plopped to the floor.

A neighborhood crowd had gathered in the gravel beyond his front yard, their pajamas and gawking faces washed in the red of Sheriff Fry's revolving sirens. He floundered at the steps, writhing about in the dirt, and cried for sheriff to put a bullet in his head, but nothing came out. They all just stood in silence and watched him burn.

Daniel Paul Bible buttoned his jeans, disappeared into the other room. After a minute, he returned to the kitchen, and tossed something at Roland. It bounced off his forehead, and fell to the floor in front of him. Without moving, Roland could see it was a quarter gram.

"Get the fuck out my house, faggot."

Bible stepped closer and kicked him in the face.

113

14

Leaving the crime scene, William interviewed neighbors that lived on Bayberry, a few blocks north from the bridge. None of the owners of the twenty-three houses he canvassed had seen or heard anything. One woman, Ms. Rita Dippel, was, however, convinced her neighbor had poisoned her dog a few months prior. She requested an inquiry into the offence. William kindly wrote down her number and said he'd send a uniformed officer out to take a statement. Later, on the other side of the street, Ms. Joanie Barter had no information regarding the crime at the river, but insisted to William that Ms. Dippel had been stealing her garden gnomes. They were gifts from her son, a traveling businessman living in the Twin Cities. One from every state. Even a few from the UK. Delaware and Florida were definitely missing and she was certain there were more. William assured her an officer would be over to look into the matter.

By noon, he'd mostly shaken the hangover, and he stopped for a cup of coffee on his way to the station. At his computer, the images from the river bubbled up from the undercurrent of his mind. He saw again the helmsman direct the boat across the water, framed by the brown river-bank and gray sky. Heard the motor as it neared him and Collette Lee. The helmsman hurdled urgently over the side of the boat before it had reached the shore, water splashing his waders. He carried the garbage bag in his hands and stomped through the water and up the rocky riverside. When he reached them, the helmsman held out the bag to Collette Lee with a look of sad terror. She simply took it from him, pulled the severed head from the last garbage bag, and set it gently on the blue tarp. Whoever did this to the girl had sawed her teeth and jaw from her head to prevent identification. Strips of gum dangled beneath a purple top lip. Riverweed clung to her white cheeks like wet twine. She could have been anywhere from sixteen to late twenties. Aquiline nose. Green eyes. Stringy red hair. A dye job—hazel roots beginning to show.

He snapped back to his computer, searched the regional missing persons and the master list of missing children.

No confident matches.

In hope of drumming up a lead, he drove north into Hegemony. There were three tattoo parlors in town—Demon Street, 420's, and Permanent Marker—but no one working at any of them recognized the picture he showed from his phone. Neither the artist responsible for the tattoo nor William's description of the girl. Most helpful was Chet, or Chud, the heavy with gauged earrings who sat behind the counter at Permanent Marker. He glanced at the photo, and then returned to his comic book, saying "No idea. Dogshit work. Whoever did that piece should be shot."

"Well, that's why I'm tracking the guy down.

Parents of the girl loved the nipple piercings, but this—"

Chet-Chud stared at him.

"So there's nothing you can tell me about this?"

"Nope. 'Spose a smart guy like you already knows it's the Two of Wands."

"The Two of Wands?"

"Yeah, the Rider-Waite."

"Rider what?"

"The tarot, man."

Of course. The tarot.

Left with no other trail, William spent two hours researching the tarot back at the office. The Two of Wands was part of the deck known as the Minor Arcana. The card depicted a page overlooking a vast landscape and ocean from a castle tower. He held a globe in one hand and a walking stick in the other. Resources agreed, at least on the broad strokes, that the card symbolized a person at the outset of a journey when an idea had been seized and a plan drafted.

William wondered what it might mean to his Jane Doe. Enough to tattoo it into her arm. Maybe she thought of herself as a seeker or an adventurer, the world at her finger tips. Or maybe she was a daydreamer that longed for escape. And, like he had been, she desparately wanted out of Black River.

Why didn't she just throw her bags in the trunk, fill up her tank at the Pump N Dump, and haul ass to Route 13 outta here?

She was caged by something. Or someone. A drunken father. A boyfriend.

Or maybe she had become her own cage— another addict with a half-hearted plan to go clean.

Maybe she was all of these things or none of them.

Maybe she got stoned one night with a wild hair up her ass, and ended up at the tattoo shop.

William went home and stood in a hot shower until the water ran cold. Then he sat in meditation for ten minutes trying to align the baboons with his breath, but they were too rambunctious to reign in, and he felt instead the onset of sleep, so he redressed in the same suit he had worn all day and ventured into the kitchen.

After a bump, and feeling particularly motivated, he decided to clean the dishes. Most of the plates had rotten food bits that had become as hard as the plate itself. He retrieved the trash bin beside the back door and one by one threw the dishes away with enough force to chip them inside the garbage bag. Then he took the whole bin outside and set it on the curb for the trash men, the sound of insects droning in his ear as the sun went down over the hill behind his apartment.

Roland inched into the steaming bath, and leaned back against the porcelain with a grunt. He draped his damaged arms on the lip of the tub, a cigarette balanced and smoking in the ashtray on the toilet a few inches from his left hand nubs. Red posies curled up from under his legs, small mushroom clouds slowly exploding in the water until the entire tub was a light hue of merlot. He sat there in silence for hours, occasionally sponging the bruises on his face, draining and refilling the tub when the water got too cold or too bloody. He'd ignore his mother's knocks at the door and her pointed requests to stop wasting water while he smoked cigarettes and filled the air with thick gray smoke. He stared at the wall in front of him as if he could see through it to some other world.

He finally emerged from the bathroom after carefully patting himself dry, shuffled downstairs—it hurt to walk—passed his mother snoring at the TV, and downstairs to his lair. He went to the back of the basement where he kept some of the things that survived the fire, and he dug out his old eight track. An archaic piece of recording equipment these days, but he had sold his computer for drugs long ago and it would work just fine. He found an unopened pack of cassettes in a box of sci-fi paperbacks and VHS tapes.

Without full fingers, his hands were too cumbersome to fret the guitar neck, but he pushed the garbage off the coffee table, and rested the guitar on its back. He tuned to open D, and using a lighter in place of a slide (he didn't own one), warmed up on some blues licks and then moved to a fuzzed out twelve bar.

He ran his old beat up SM57 to his amp's sweet spot (remembering it was bottom left corner), popped a new cassette into the eight track, and hit record. From there, he left structure behind and simply layered sounds——warbling feedback, pick scrapes, random fret noise and harmonics. On one track, Roland beat the strings to create a percussive pattern. On another, he recorded delayed glissandos. He wasn't consciously planning anything. He just allowed the ideas to pass through him onto the tape before rewinding the whole thing to add another piece to the orchestration. At some point, a languid melody emerged—a single note slide line that pinned the entire piece down.

When he deemed it complete, he relaxed on the couch with his headphones and listened to it repeatedly while he smoked a bit of the bag he had procured earlier that day. Shortly after, he noticed the morning sun creep into the basement windows.

William tailed Fry's Jeep up a set of tracks through tall grass to a lone trailer surrounded by sugar maple and rock elm. The sheriff pulled into the grass and parked beside the rusted body of a 1969 AMC Rebel. William stopped behind him and turned off the ignition.

"Mailman said it's somewhere here in the front yard," Fry said when William caught up to him.

The Air Streamer looked like a soda can kicked around for four decades.

"There," William said, pointing casually to a lifeless body laying face up in the brown grass.

Snapping on a pair of latex gloves, he squatted near the body. Faded prison tattoos—swastikas, Parteiadlers, spider webs—and dozens of deep gashes marked the man's shirtless torso. Both sides of his neck carried SS Runes. Bashed-in teeth and a deathblow to his forehead made it impossible to discern the man's age. Or facial features.

"Jesus," Fry whispered to himself.

A few feet from the body, William spotted a shotgun, *White Justice* whittled into the stock.

"Cute." William pointed again.

Sheriff Fry shook off a laugh.

119

"They gave him gills."

"Yeah, looks like we got a real Conan the Barbarian." Fry glanced left. "William." He took a step back. Then another. "Shit, William—look out!"

William looked up.

A malnourished pit bull growled as it ran full-throttle toward him, its gigantic paws clomping in the dirt. Behind it trailed a heavy chain leash. He secured the taser from his breast pocket. The dog hurtled forward.

William fired.

The taser sounded like an electric insect as its electrodes connected with the dog's head. The dog rifled past, knocking into William's shoulder, and skid to a stop.

William got to his feet and approached the dog. It lay on its side, breathing gently.

"You ought not be pokin' with any limbs you wanna keep," sheriff warned.

"He'll be sleepin' for awhile."

He leaned down and lifted the chain. It wound back into the bushes next to the trailer. He followed it.

"Where you goin'?"

William elbowed through the bushes into the backyard. The chain had worn ligature marks into a tree. He took stock of the area. Grass grew intermittently among dirt and dog shit. A shed, older and twice the length of the trailer, rested half-hidden by more bushes and copse. William checked for another dog, and when he didn't spot one, he sidestepped the shit to the shed.

Ammonia permeated its interior. He covered his nose and mouth with a handkerchief from his jacket. Obligatory cook essentials—Iodine jugs, match strips, empty Sudafed packets, Drano, Lye—loaded a nearby workbench. Spiro piping, suspended above by twine, coiled to a hole in the ceiling. The drywall, blackened by smoke damage and burned away in places, exposed charred and flaked 2-by-4s. Whenever the fire started, it hadn't stopped the kitchen. The floor was still filthy from ash and remains of the wall, but newer garbage—plastic bags, junk food wrappers, soda bottles, lighters, and newspaper—had been discarded more recently. William slogged through the ruin to a Louvre side door.

He hesitated there for a moment, finally peeping between the door slats, and then he unhooked the latch and stepped into a second area hidden by an encircling thicket. In front of him was a dirt ring approximately two feet down and six feet in diameter. A dead dog lay on the far side, blood-stained dirt beneath it.

At the other end of the ring, directly across from him, were a dozen stacked dog cages, empty except four. One housed another pit bull, grey with white scars across its withers, which hadn't stopped barking at William since he came through the door. Judging by their fearful eyes and size, the other three were fodder.

"Another fine pastime of our magnificent citizens." Fry leaned out from the door jamb, his voice startling William. "Seems it's become more prevalent in the last ten years. We'll call animal control, but you should come take a look at this."

William spit. "There's more?"

The Airstream was a garbage dump of a living space. That said, the place had been ransacked. Every cabinet opened, canned food thrown to the floor. The intruder had emptied the under bed storage and scattered clothes about the place. Ripped apart with its stuffing pulled out, a mattress rested upright against the wall. At the dinette, there was a second male victim, head drooped back on the cushion. Dried blood ran from a deep gash in his neck down to the front of his t-shirt.

"Well, yeah, there's him and his minor flesh wound," Fry said. He beckoned William from the door. "But here . . . ."

William stepped to the stove. Arranged in a circle on the small countertop were five or six teeth with strands of gum still attached. "Here we go." William cracked a smile.

"Right? If that ain't enough . . . ."

Fry tugged on the refrigerator handle. William ducked down to look inside. Next to a six pack of PBR and a bottle of mustard was a human hand inside a clear plastic bag.

William sat at his computer screen, scratching quick notes into his memo pad. Fry entered his office. William pointed at the screen. "Recognize this dude?"

"The scumbag on the couch?"

"The other one."

"No wonder I didn't place him."

William scrolled down the record. "Name is Randall Lee Wise. From Louisville. He's collected a shitload of arrests there going back to his teens." He skimmed the screen. "Various assaults, drunk and disorderly, animal neglect, carrying a weapon without a permit, an OWI, possession . . . blah, blah, blah. Nothing

122

here to suggest he's our guy."

"Just the usual asshole."

"Yeah, other than that, he's been linked to various white supremacy groups in Kentucky. No surprise there either, considering his affinity for Third Reich ink. Not even a speeding ticket here in Iowa."

"Maybe he was turning over a new leaf. Wanted to try something new. And his friend on the couch? He looked vaguely familiar."

"He's a local kid. Tyler Youngs. Ring a bell?"

"Hard to keep track of every fallen robin. Toss a stone and you'll hit a tweaker. Should I know him?"

"Let's see . . ." William clicked on the kid's file. "Looks like he's been popular with Black River PD. And his pals . . ." He scrolled past Tyler's photo and rap sheet—a non-descript mether with a slew of meth-related charges—to his known associates. "Holy shit." William rocketed from his slouched posture. He looked at Fry. "Roland Jarzenbowski. I grew up with him."

"Really. I did not know that. Still in touch?"

"No, haven't seen him in ten years. Maybe longer."

Fry raised his eyebrows.

"What?" William asked, sipping his coffee.

"You haven't seen him around town?"

"No, not that I remember."

"Oh, you'd remember."

15

William didn't recognize Sheryl Jarzenbowski when she answered the door on the second knock, and he hesitated for a moment, mumbling to himself and rechecking the address from the memo pad in his hands. Her face was harder—pruned on the sides by crow's feet and speckled with age spots, her shoulder length hair now grey and unwashed and broken into brittle pieces with split ends, her mouth wrinkled from smoking. She was never beautiful, but the years spent as a bar stool bunny had taken their toll and weighed on her now tenfold. The blue eyes, however, had somehow retained the insolubility he remembered.

"Sheryl?"

"Was wondering when you'd grace us with your presence." She wasn't smiling.

There would be no heartfelt hug. That was to be expected—she never liked him. Even as a child he felt unwelcome in their home. The reason had eluded him until sometime in high school, when he asked Roland why.

"I dunno, man. She's traditional," Roland had said, looking away like he always did when he was uncomfortable.

As cryptic as it was, William had puzzled out the meaning.

"Roland in?"

"And if I said he wasn't?"

"I'd go and sit in my car and wait til he was."

"Might be waiting a long time."

William shrugged. "Good for me he's home then."

"Well, hurry in before you let the cats out."

She wore a bathrobe and faded pink slippers with tube socks. He followed her down the hall, three cats skirting past them. In the living room, a TV aired some daytime talk show, one of those newly formatted jobs with the five hosts. Amazing how little so many had to say.

"I don't like to answer the door. I got bad circulation."

As they came to the kitchen, the stench of cat piss and rot hit William, and he considered the possibility that Roland might still be cooking. Then he saw the garbage bags and cat litter in the side foyer.

"You catch the bastard that killed Frank and his brother?"

"Not yet."

"Ain't that why they hired you?"

She stopped at a door next to the refrigerator, hacking into her fleeced elbow. Then, swinging the door open, she yelled, "Rollie—you got company."

"Thanks, Sheryl. It was good to see you again."

She didn't respond, simply turned and walked back toward the living room.

125

He set off down into the dark, wincing every time the wooden stairs creaked beneath his weight. He wanted to descend quietly, though he wasn't sure why.

That wasn't true.

Fry's account of the fire had unsettled him. He tried to imagine what his old friend looked like, wondered if the monstrosity the sheriff had described matched reality. And for whatever reason, he approached this drop-in like he was visiting the sick or the dying in the hospital. Hush, hush. The invalid is suffering.

But there was something else, too.

Once, he was closer to Roland than anyone else in his life. They were brothers. In a lot of ways, he'd never been as close to anyone since. Not even his ex-wife. There had never been an inciting incident that led to the dissolution between him and Roland. Simply two trajectories headed in different directions. Their bond occupied a specific place in time: the awkward period of early adolescence to high school graduation. And like all childhood things, it necessarily needed to be packaged away. Hadn't it? Time had irreconcilably eroded their friendship. What did they possibly have in common now? Roland was a reminder of just how far the world was moving away from him.

He reached the bottom of the stairs, and turned into the room, all at once hyperconscious of his physicality, which compelled him to thumb his nose awkwardly as if he had an itch there, and then thrust his hands into his jacket pockets and exhale like he'd just finished a five-mile run.

"Look what came home to roost." Roland hunched forward on the couch, all glassy bloodshot eyes and twitching legs.

The only light were the slats coming through the basement windows. William could still make out his disfigured face.

"How you doin', Roland."

"You know, Willie . . . same as it ever was." He rubbed the top of his head. "Got a facelift."

"I see that." William edged into the room. "Looks great. Much improved."

A smile splayed Roland's discolored cheek, affecting a Chelsea grin that ran up the right side of his face. With the shadows, his head was half a withered jack o lantern. He pulled from his cigarette, snug between his thumb and middle nub, and expelled the smoke with a chuckle. "That's—I like tha—that's rich."

William noticed the guitar on the coffee table.

"So you're still playin'?"

"Well—no, I mean—I played—yeah, I've had to change—lay it flat like a lap steel, you know, like—play it with a slide." He wiggled the nubs on his hand. "My—I can't—the neck—with these things I can't fret no more."

When they were sixteen, they had skipped school and drove up to Hegemony for the day. At a pawn shop, Roland fell in love for the first time. She was a black Les Paul Custom. Maple neck. Humbuckers. Fuckin' raw power. He had worked every overtime shift at Mickey D's to save for the guitar.

But like most first loves, it wasn't in the cards. By the time he got the money together and made it back to the shop, someone had already snagged her. William thought Roland would cry right there in the store. He had settled for a beat up Strat. Even enough money left over

127

for a decent amp.

Up until that point, Roland had cut his teeth on an old piece of shit acoustic he found at an auction. He spent most of the next year in his room. William could drop by anytime and find him practicing—learning licks, running scales, playing along to their favorite records. Soon he had his own riffs, which eventually grew into songs. And they were good.

That was the thing about Roland. No matter what he was into—if he was really into it—he breathed it. It became air to him.

"You still have the old Strat?"

Roland's eyes fell to the table. "No, it got burnnn—its gaw—I lost it."

"You playin' out at all?"

"Nah—I wish, I wish I had—I just—all I do now is, uh—solo—I started recording some stuff. Just me though."

"Songs?"

"Yeah—kinda—I guess—maybe."

"I'd love to hear 'em sometime."

"Well—I've got a—there's one I did last—"

"Definitely. Some other time. I'm actually here because—"

"Oh, right. Right on." Roland fiddled with his face.

"I've gotta ask you some questions."

"Shoot."

"You know Tyler Youngs?"

"Wha—what about him?"

"He turned up at a homicide earlier today."

"I mean—you must have—Tyler's a good du—a

nice guy. It wasn't Tyler. He's got no prob—he doesn't—he minds—he doesn't have beef with anybody."

"No, he turned up at a homicide . . . as a victim."

"What?"

"I'm sorry."

"Wha—I mean—that can't—I just saw him—we had a drink last week—that's fucked, man."

"There was another victim." William dug into his jacket pocket, and handed Roland a mug shot of Randy Lee Wise.

"An—that's what's his na—what's-his-fuck—" Roland seemed to be searching some filing cabinet in his brain. "Ray. That's the du—that's the guy's name."

"Ray?"

"Nah—wait—not—Ran—Randall something. Yeah, Randall. I—I—met him a few—once or twice. I didn't like—no friend of mine. Came outta—just showed up—Tyler met him at the Rock Bottom, I think. He was—one of—Nazi—one of those assholes—all that white power bullshit. Shitheel."

"And Tyler?"

"Tyler. Nah, man. One of the few friends I still have."

"So what was their connection?"

"Dunno."

"Come on, Roland. I was in the shed. Bit strange. Tyler Goodboy hangin' with trash like Randy Lee."

"Why would I—I have no reason to lie to you, dude. Maybe they were fuu—swapping fluids. I dunno. Why would I—I don't care. I mind my own. It's not a stret—If I had to guess—probably—obviously—they were cooking. Seems pretty self-explan—evident,

129

Detective Wolfe."

They were silent for a moment.

"All right," William said, mindful of his tone. "How'd you get that shiner?"

Roland stared off into the dark. "How'd you get yours?"

Tyler Youngs' apartment would have been a gold mine if William was looking for porn or video games, but it was a bust in providing any breadcrumbs.

He delivered propane and petroleum for Landon & Sons Fuel. William stopped there and spoke with the owner and a few co-workers that were friends with him. By all accounts, he was a solid worker who went MIA a month before. No call, no show. He turned his back on thirty grand a year, full benefits, and a 401k. It'd seem something pretty profitable was on his horizon.

Or he was a dumbass.

No one at Landon & Sons recognized Randy Lee's mug shot. If the two set up shop together, Tyler kept it to himself.

Apparently, the kid wasn't a total dumbass. Loose lips sank ships.

Then again, other ships sank ships, too.

Shortly after the Rock Bottom opened for happy hour, William strode through the front door, reinvigorated from the Adderall he dropped forty minutes before. He clomped over peanut shells to the bar. Two men sat at the far end, watching TV and talking amongst themselves. The bartender, a blonde in her mid-fifties, approached William.

"We've got dollar drafts and two dollar Captain n Cokes til six," she said.

"Thank you, but no." He flashed his badge. "Detective William Wolfe."

"Delilah. What can I help ya with?"

"Have you seen either of these men?"

William tossed Tyler and Randy Lee's mug shots onto the bar.

"That's Tyler," she said without picking up the photos. "He's a regular. Why? Has he done somethin' wrong?"

"Probably. He's dead."

"What? How?" She wiped her hands on a bar towel.

"He was murdered. Along with this other guy. You know him?"

"Said his name was Steve."

"Steve?"

"Yeah. He started showing up about a month ago. Maybe two months. From outta town. Creepy guy. I didn't like him."

"You ever see them together?"

"I don't recall. I don't think so."

"But you talked to him?"

"A little. Like I said, he wasn't from here, and I didn't like the cut of his jib. Not many did. Made people uneasy. Said he was in town helping a friend or something."

"You remember his name?"

"I don't. I'm sorry."

"Well, thank you for your time."

William scrawled his number into his memo pad, ripped the page out, and handed it to Delilah. "In case you remember anything."

She smiled, showing her teeth. He tried to hide any revulsion, but it must have shown on his face. She quickly tightened her lips and walked to the other end of the bar.

Outside the bar, William's phone rang.

"Where you at?" the sheriff asked when he answered.

"Rock Bottom. Following up on Tyler Youngs and Randy Lee."

"Anything good?"

"No."

"I got something that'll make you smile."

"All right. Shoot."

"Prints on the hand belong to a girl named Rosemary Montgomery."

"And?"

"And I been rackin' my brain for the last four hours tryin' to remember why the name sounded familiar. Then I remembered. Night of the fire, me and Widy go to the hospital. When we arrived, Roland's fiancé was there—
—"

"And her name's Rosemary Montgomery."

"Indeed, it was. Same as our Jane Doe. I remember those green eyes. I'm on my way to pick him up now."

"I'll meet you back at the station."

"You spoke to him today?"

"Yeah, nothing there either but he's got a cut over

132

his eye."

"Fuck me. That's happening to everyone these days. Wonder how he got his?"

William didn't respond.

"You want me to take the interview?" Fry asked.

"Nah, I got it. But you're wrong."

"About what?"

"This doesn't make me smile."

16

Roland sat in the basement for awhile after William left, smoking and playing slide licks on his guitar. It wasn't until after noon that he went upstairs. He grabbed a Mountain Dew from the refrigerator and walked to the front of the house to find out if the mail had arrived.

"Roland? What'd William want?"

He cracked the door, reached an arm outside, and opened the metal mailbox mounted to the house. Sandwiched between a Valu-Save coupon pack and the month's electric bill was his disability check. His cracked smile creased the side of his face.

Hallelujah.

He stood at the door and marveled at the check for a moment like it was the Eighth Wonder of the World.

"Roland?" his mother called from the living room.

"I don't—I have no idea."

"Well, what did he say?"

"I—Goddamn it—I'm—busy—Mother."

"'Scuse me for livin'."

He marched to the kitchen, dug around in the

silverware drawer for a knife, and slit open the envelope. Every month it was the same, but every month it was like seeing it again for the first time. Fifteen hundred sixty three dollars and nineteen cents.

Roland decided right then that he was gonna splurge. No reason to feel guilty about it either. The last week had been a fecal storm, and he deserved to cut loose a bit. He carefully folded the check and secured it in his pocket.

Putting the knife back, he noticed someone had taken out the garbage.

Roland spent most of the afternoon trekking around town. His body was still sore from his run-in with Bible, but the promise of a big score kept his spirits up. He'd never used a savings account—didn't trust banks— so first step was Fareway's customer service department. Checks Now charged fifteen percent on all checks cashed versus Fareway's five dollar fee. No brainer. While he was in the store he picked up another Mountain Dew and a Star Crunch for lunch.

In the checkout lane—behind a woman and her daughter who tried pretending he wasn't there, uncomfortably unloading the contents of their cart onto the belt—he felt the eyes of the Shadow People on him. One to his left peered at him from the edge of an end cap of Lay's potato chips. Another from two checkout lanes to the right.

Only a nanosecond—they darted away before he could identify them for sure.

Not spooked enough to ruin his day, Roland hustled over to Biscuits' place, feeling for his wallet several times along the way, for some reason afraid he'd find it'd disappeared before he could score.

His friend had been busy at the kitchen table with his miniatures when he arrived, black metal on in the living room. Biscuit was a Luddite. Totally against modern video games, he loved Dungeons & Dragons, and if he wasn't playing or designing dungeons, he was painting figures. He owned a two and half inch magnifying glass, one used for soldering with alligator clips mounted on four-way swivels, and he'd spend hours hunched over the magnifying glass, applying meticulously placed coats of paint to plastic fantasy creatures. Two dozen half-painted orcs, tiny jars of acrylic paint, and brushes rested next to the dismantled stereo. Apparently, Biscuits had given up on his quest to remove the FBI bugs from his electrics. Or the voices stopped.

"Dig the new army? I mixed a tank green with a little more grey for their flesh tone. The results are astounding. These guys look fuckin' fierce. So sick. I can't wait to premiere them at tomorrow night's session. They're gonna tear the party a new asshole."

"Cool."

"Sure you can't make it?"

Roland had tried to sit in on a session once. He'd been too tweaked to learn the rules, and was too indecisive on his turns, the options too much of a burden, which caused the other players to become annoyed with him. Killing shit and looting ancient treasure had its charm, but the party members' bad British accents and high fantasy speak was embarrassing. Fine—they were nerds, but did they need to shove it in your face?

"No—I mean—I can—I've got—I'm kinda in a hurry."

"Right-o." Biscuit hopped up from the table and sprinted to the bedroom.

Roland rolled through the house and down to his lair, stripping off the sweat drenched hoodie and t-shirt and throwing them to the floor. He popped to the couch and ran a celebratory flame to foil, a great wave elevating him to the throne of gods. He turned up Motorhead on the stereo, nabbed a garbage bag from upstairs, and threw away every can, plastic bottle, junk food wrapper, empty cigarette box, used tissue, and half-eaten microwave dinner. Charging up the stairs, Roland continued his cleaning spree and threw away all the cereal and pre-made food boxes. Then he sprayed the counters and table with Lysol and wiped them down with paper towels. He filled the sink with hot water, scrubbing the rot and hardened food from every fork, spoon, bowl, plate, and pan.

"Roland, could you turn that music down? I can't hear my show."

The TV volume rose in living room.

He moved on to the side foyer, dumped the litter box into the trash—gagging as he did—and then swept up all the rogue turds, loose litter, and bits of cat food. He mopped the floor and refilled the box with fresh litter. Finally, he took the garbage out to the alley and heaved it into the black Roughneck.

Just as he re-entered the house, there was a knock at the door. He heard his mother swear and get up.

She opened the door.

"Sheriff Fry. Is there something wrong?"

Hollis Fry escorted Roland to the back of the Jeep. Neither attempted small talk as the sheriff pulled from the curb.

Three boys, the ones Roland saw earlier in the week, stood on the corner and watched the police vehicle. As the sheriff turned left onto Brown Deer Road, he casually waved to them. The boys didn't wave back.

Roland glanced out the window to spot the Mexican boy's gaze locked on him.

At a metal table anchored to the interview room wall, Roland quaked from the methamphetamine, arms jerking out occasionally like he had an extreme case of hiccups. His eyes darted from the white ceiling tile to the green walls. He tried not to look, but found himself coming back to the camera mounted in the corner and pointed directly at him. They were watchin' him. Fuckin' with him and watchin' him. He'd been stewing for twenty minutes and after ten he was ready to gouge out his eyes and scratch at the walls. What were they playing at?

Several more minutes came and went, and he started beating the table.

"Come—Come on, man. I can't sit—I got shit to do."

Less than sixty seconds later, William entered the room.

"Bout time."

"Sorry, I was reviewing something. You goin' stir crazy in here?"

"Yeah, man."

"Did you want anything? Water? Soda?"

"A cigarette."

"Wish I could help you. I could use one myself."

"So what—I mean—why am I—I thought we already went over this—through this."

"We did and we didn't."

"What so—I'm a—you think I had—I killed Tyler and that other dude?"

"I dunno. I just have to ask these questions."

"You don't—I mean—how can you—you don't know? Really? Is this really yo—William Wolfe I'm talkin—speaking to?"

"I'm just doing my job."

"Right."

"So when was the last time you saw Tyler?"

"A few weeks ago. May—Maybe."

"You two ever fight?"

"No, man—I already—he didn't have beef with any—anybody."

"You never had an argument . . . over tweak? Maybe he owed you money? You owed him money?"

"It wasn't like that. We just—we were bar friends."

"Meaning?"

"We hung—we'd shoot the shit at the bar—hang out and drink."

"So you never went to his place or he to yours."

"No. I mean—it wasn't—I don't have—I don't like people over at my mom's."

"So he didn't know any of your other friends?"

"No—who?—I mean—not that I know of."

"What about old friends?"

"What?"

"Ex-girlfriends?"

"No—why?"

"Four days ago a body was found along Black River."

"Okay. So—"

"It was Rosemary."

William continued to talk, but the sound of his voice receded. A shrill buzz rose in pitch.

When Roland came to William had him pinned against the wall. Sheriff Fry was behind him. A horrible sound filled the room. Like something dying. It took him a moment to realize it was his voice. He was screaming.

"Lemme get the cuffs on 'im," the sheriff said.

"No, it's fine. I'm fine. Roland, I need you to calm down. Can you just breathe for a second?"

The screaming stopped. He concentrated on his breath. He inhaled and exhaled. There were tears on his face.

"Can you sit down for me, Roland?"

He did as William asked.

"I'm gonna get you a drink of water. I'll be right back. It's important you stay seated. Okay?"

Roland didn't answer.

"Can I trust you to stay seated?"

"Yes."

William followed the sheriff from the room.

Roland's mind warbled like Jell-O. A couple minutes later, William returned with a glass of water.

"Water's—I can't stand—I'm not thirsty."

"Just in case."

William set the glass on the table.

"I'm sorry, Roland."

"Can I—I'd like to—are we done here?"

"Almost. I was wonderin' if you could tell me a little about Rosemary."

"Like what?"

"When was the last time you saw her?"

"I—I—I didn't kill her."

"Didn't say you did. But I want to find out who did. Any information you could provide may help."

"It's been—I haven't seen her in over—in a year or so. Not since she bail—since we broke up."

That was a lie. He'd seen her two weeks before. Some days he'd wake with restlessness in his marrow, find himself roaming the streets. He'd look up and be across the street from Los Portales, waiting to catch a glimpse of her.

"She leave on good terms?"

"No. She was—there was somebody else."

"Who?"

"Dunno. It was—there were—it kinda like—bit of a crowded playin' field."

"You ever want to lash out. Get even. Show the bitch what's up?"

Roland scrunched his brow. "Come—come on now. Seriously?"

"Are you still in love with her?"

"Does it—what difference does it make?"

"What else can you tell me about her?"

"That's what I'm saying. Nothing. Haven't seen 'er. Heard she was working at Los Portales. That's it."

"The Mexican restaurant?"

It'd been four hours since they'd released him and Black River's streets were dark. Sweating inside his hoodie, he walked purposefully, the tangle in his heart driving his ramshackle body to its limits. He was merely a passenger at this point, only vaguely aware of his surroundings. Past the ball diamond—never played a game in his life, would rather watch paint dry—he cut through Highland Park, and made his way east on Scott.

He'd never been much for daytime. Night, on the other hand, was full of possibility. No matter how tired he'd been during the day, twilight always reinvigorated him. Everything happened after sunset. Everything that mattered anyway. There was the neon life, but it was something more. Some elemental energy in the air. He'd always felt most alive, his imagination most fertile, after the world went to bed. Even in the days before he had hair on his balls, he'd stay up drawing in a spiral bound notebook under his blankets with a flashlight, waiting for his mother to get home from the bar on a week night. He got lost in worlds of his own making where time raced by. The next day at school, he'd fight to stay awake in class. The days of his education passed this way, dissolving like scenes in an art film, one into the next, without much context or meaning.

At the end of Scott, Roland turned onto Route 7. The lack of street lights made walking this stretch dangerous at night. The river's breeze felt good on his cheeks, and, perhaps because it was so dark, he pulled back his hood to air out the rest of his face. The bridge was a half mile up on the left. William's words came back to him. Then the image of her body along the banks of Black River. He was tired—a stitch in his side drove him to carry all his weight on his right, dragging his other half like a zombie—and a wheeze broke into a fit of coughing, but his anger borne him forward. White lights of a lone car careened by him into the night beyond. As the car passed, Roland wished it would have collided into him, vaulting him into the ditch.

Maybe he'd get lucky, be impaled on a random fence post or rusty rebar.

It took him fifteen minutes to reach the bridge's stop lights. He struggled up the walkway using the iron railing for support. Halfway across, he stopped and leaned toward the river. His heart drummed in his chest. He felt faint and nauseous. Dropping his head into his arms, he concentrated on the sound of the river. When the sickness passed, Roland cocked his head toward the dark motion below. Listened to its arcane blues come down the line.

In a way, she had died when she left him. He'd been living in the memories of her for over a year. Did she know her killer? Did she go peacefully? He told himself he wished she had, but beneath that thought there was another uglier truth. A part of him hoped she suffered. She deserved it. She was like him. Born to night. Drawn to its dark places, its promises of fantasy and thrill, its ability to nurture and conceal. Drawn to its tendency to destroy. He tried to shake the thought and

143

the guilt away, but it lodged there in his mind like a canker-worm.

He heard the grass rustle below. Someone walked in shadow along the bank and then disappeared under the bridge. For a moment, the silhouette reminded him of the Mexican boy.

17

Los Portales' lunch rush consisted of three customers. Two men bobbed over plates of refried beans and enchiladas. They ate hurriedly, their knotty workman's hands cutting and shoveling fork loads into their mouths like they hadn't eaten in days. Maybe the food was that good. An older woman drank coffee and read a paper, the check on the table.

Die-cut paper picado flags and plastic accordion banners dangled from the Talavera tiled ceiling. Brightly painted clay masks—deer, bull, hyena—hung from the walls with outstretched tongues. One of them, a horned demon encircled by a two-headed snake that expelled fire from a mouthful of fangs, commanded the main terra cotta dining wall. The wall itself had a painted representation of a Vision Serpent. William remembered his mother once had him study Mayan culture. A part of their bloodletting rituals, the Vision Serpent was a gateway into the spirit realm, where ancestors or gods emerged from the serpent's mouth. For the participant, these visions were a kind of communion with the gods.

Perhaps the strange choice in dining ambience explained the lack of business.

A Mexican woman greeted him at the register.

"¿Cómo está usted?" She smiled broadly, picking up a menu. "Espanol?"

He knew what was coming next.

"No Espanol."

Her smile waned. "Oh."

William was a constant disappointment. He flashed his badge. "Anyone here close with Rosemary Montgomery?"

"Si—yes—Kara." She pointed to the bar archway.

Kara had a ponytail that bounced as she seesawed from the ice machine—filling a six inch food pan with ice—to a sink behind the counter. Lost in the work, or pretending to be, she didn't make eye contact when William approached.

"May need a bigger bucket," he said as cordial as possible.

She regarded him as one would a turd in the toilet first thing in the morning. Her doe eyes were anything but naïve. She sighed inaudibly, seeming to collect herself before answering.

"Yeah . . ." She mumbled something William couldn't catch. "Did you need something?"

"Detective William Wolfe. Can I speak to you for a minute?"

Kara puckered her lips around a Newport and took in a long drag, shuffling her weight from foot to foot as if trying to get warm in the alley behind the restaurant.

"We went to high school together in Hegemony.

146

She needed a place to crash for a bit. You know how that goes—a couple weeks turned into a year. We were friends, but I didn't see her a whole lot. Here mostly . . . when she showed up."

"So she moved into your place after she left Roland?"

"Yeah, that guy's a freak."

"How so?"

"Have you seen him?"

William didn't respond.

"Besides, he'd stalk her. He'd stand across the street out front if she was working. Sometimes if she wasn't. Just stand there looking. It was creepy."

"He ever threaten her?"

"Not that I know of. One time he did come into the restaurant. Fernando, one of the cooks, had to escort him out."

"What did he do?"

"I dunno. The usual take me back bullshit. It was embarrassing. And sad. I felt bad for her."

"Was he ever violent when they were together?"

"We hadn't reconnected at that point, but I know they argued a lot. Rosemary could be pretty crazy herself. She was always in some kind of turmoil in high school. And I don't think she ever really moved beyond that. Some people just feed off chaos. It was hard to get close to her, to know who she really was."

"So you didn't party with her?"

"I loved Rosemary, but she was like the Titanic—I didn't wanna go down with her."

"You know any names of friends, acquaintances?"

"I don't know. I'm sorry. I can't recall anybody

147

specifically in the last year."

"Her stuff still at your place?"

"She didn't have a lot. What she did have, she kept in her car. Still sitting in the driveway."

William leaned against Rosemary's 1983 Ford Escort, jimmying the orange driver's side door, and swearing under his breath. He jiggled the Slim Jim a few more times before the lock finally clicked. Trash bags bulging with clothes filled the backseat. Some so full the plastic was ripping. Others puked out jeans and halters. A toaster and desk lamp had been lost among the bags. An old record player and a plastic crate of LPs were crammed between the seat and floor.

William opened the door and sifted through the receipts, cellophane wrappers, and cigarette packs on the passenger side floor. In the glove compartment, he found another opened cigarette pack. He flipped back the top. A few grams of tweak. Dropping the little baggie into his left breast pocket, he backed out the car and hit Hollis on speed dial.

"Shoot," the sheriff answered.

"Can you send a tow truck out to Malibu Heights?"

Within an hour and a half, William had unloaded all the clothes from the trash bags and sorted and folded them out onto a table in the station's garage. He'd triple-checked every pocket, only to find two dimes, a nickel, five pennies, and a half-eaten roll of breath mints. The record crate contained mostly jazz and old RnB, but there was also a vinyl titled *Shaky Hands* by a band called the Occupants. Not recognizing the name, William had flipped over the record and discovered Roland listed on guitar. He'd made a note to spin it when there was free time. Then he tracked down a cardboard box and collected all the garbage and paper from the car's floor and took the box and the Occupants' record to his office.

At his desk, William examined the contents of the box, separating all the crumpled receipts into a small pile. He flipped through the receipts a few times and then put the pile into a plastic bag. He stuffed all the cellophane, cigarette packs, and other trash into another bag and tossed it back into the box. Among the trash, he discovered a phone number written on a ripped piece of paper. No name, just a number. He copied the number into his notepad and stored the piece of paper in a third bag. He leaned back in his chair and stared at the bags.

He had been sitting there for some time, his head propped in his hand, when Darwin Cash came to his door.

"We got shots fired over on Halstead."

Halstead. Big Deal's street.

William jolted from his seat. As he reached the door, his phone rang. He turned back to his desk and scooped the receiver to his ear.

"Hello?"

Dial tone.

He slammed the receiver down, reached into his jacket, and yanked out his cell as it rang and vibrated in his hand.

"William, it's your father—"

149

"Now's not a good time."

"She's gone." Lionel was crying.

"What?"

"I can't find her. She's gone."

Lionel was pacing the kitchen when William and Darwin Cash entered the house.

"I just left for a bit. We needed a few things from Milde's. She was sleeping. I thought it would be fine."

"How's she been the last few days?"

"Same. Hardly eating. When she's awake she doesn't talk."

William nodded. "Stay here. We'll find her."

"I'm coming with."

"You need to be here case she comes back." He put a hand on Lionel's shoulder. "It's gonna be okay, dad."

Outside William told Darwin Cash to search out along the road that passed the Stephenson field, if need be they'd walk the aisles of dead stalks later. Then William waded into the foxtail barley and the bur bristlegrass toward the copse beyond the barn.

Sheriff Fry's boots clomped across the hardwood of the living room. He paused at the archway to the kitchen, pulled up his sagging Wranglers, and sighed. Jesus Christ. He stepped into the room and hunkered down on a knee. Norman Eckels, or whatever the hell he called himself, lay splayed out on the vinyl flooring with a pistol near his hand, the back of his head blown off. The

150

wall behind him looked like a goddamned Pollock. He ran a finger over the overturned tabletop next to the boy. Licked it.

He studied the scene for a moment, and then, grumbling, he rose from his knee, and walked back to the front door, and climbed into his Jeep in the driveway. He retrieved his phone from the passenger seat and dialed.

Leon Hutchins picked up on the third ring.

"Looks like your boy went and lost his mind," sheriff said.

"Eh?"

"Big Dipshit or whatever. At his place now. Whoever did it left a mess."

"What about my shit?"

"Nothing here."

Leon went ape shit, cussing and growling so loud sheriff had to yank the phone from his ear. He looked into the rearview mirror and spotted the crime scene van pulling into the drive behind him.

"This is gettin' outta hand now. You need to end this quick and quiet."

"Workin' on it." Leon spit the words out like they were bad take out.

"Work faster."

Sheriff ended the call and stepped out of the Jeep to greet Collette Lee with a smile.

As he reached the top of a small incline made slippery by rain, William pushed against the trunk of a silver maple and stepped over a fallen branch, his muddy foot disappearing back into the blanket of yellow and red

151

leaves. Initially, he left the farm with no destination, but there in that moment, listening to the hollow whooshing sound that followed his footsteps and echoed among the leafless trees as he walked, he realized intuition was leading him to the creek.

Sara often took him there as a child. An abandoned car—decades of rust and a gutted out interior—served as a playground for his imagination. A few yards behind it a thick rope dangled from a massive oak branch that arched over the small creek. He had lost himself in many solo adventures—most of them accompanied by a *twootwoo-twootwoo-twootwoo-two* of machine gun fire—where he transformed the car into various vehicles, secret hideouts, and treasure-filled archeological sites. Other times he'd grab the rope, and swing across the creek, imploring his mother to check out what a badass he was, shouting things like, "Did you see that one, mom?" or "Hey, mom, watch this!" and she'd look up from her book and say "Wwwwooow!" or "William, please be careful."

He marched to the creek, and then continued along its edge at a brisk pace, certain now that he would find her at their old spot. He gazed down into the creek bed. The drop here a good ten feet, lined on both sides by fallen trees and savage roots that jutted from the earth. There was no water at the bottom, only rock and muddy pools that radiated damp cold and melancholy.

Soon enough he came upon her.

She sat on a giant log with her back to him, wearing a white nightgown. In front of her the old car sat camouflaged against the leaves. Beyond, the oak still remained, but the rope had become sickly–looking, like a single strand of Spanish moss. She seemed rapt by something on the other side of the creek, something in the distance, out beyond the trees along the horizon.

Not wanting to startle her, William slowed, but she heard his approach, and she turned. There was no recognition in her eyes.

"Good afternoon."

He smiled and said, "Howdy. I'm sorry. I didn't mean to frighten you."

"Oh, no, you haven't."

"Good. I'm glad." He didn't stop walking until he made his way around the log and to the car. He stood for a moment at the passenger side with his hands in his coat. The soles of his shoes had accumulated an inch and a half of sludge, and not knowing what to say, he began to scrape them off against the front wheel well. He looked over at her bare feet caked in mud. "It's a bit crisp out today."

"It's not too bad."

When he finished his task, William stepped toward her.

"You mind?" he said, pointing to the log.

She shook her head and returned her gaze to the horizon. Before he sat, he took off his jacket and gently put it around her shoulders. If she noticed, she didn't seem to mind.

"My son plays here," she said.

They sat there for sometime in silence, Sara staring out as she had been and William trying to remember his grand afternoon epics when he was the hero of his own tales.

18

The Jamboree Showroom was located on the westside of Hegemony, sandwiched between Synthetix Production Company and Quality Laundry Service. The car lot held nearly 1,295 used vehicles, or at least that's what Jamby the TV mascot claimed on the commercials. In actuality it was closer to nine hundred at one time, but who was counting? Smoke and mirrors. They were in the business of selling fantasy. And really the entire existence of The Jamboree Showroom was complete fantasy. The owner, who appeared in the commercials alongside Jamby sporting a well-groomed mustache and toupee, went by Jimbo Jamboree. But that wasn't his real name. Apparently, Tyco Cooter didn't have the right star quality for the used car business. Beyond that, he wasn't even the owner. At least not anymore.

Some years back, Mr. Jamboree decided he'd supplement his income with a second business in meth manufacture. Problem was, as Esmeralda would make clear, he'd encroached on her territory. She sent out Leon and Carlos. They gagged and blindfolded him, threw him in the trunk, and drove him out into a field in the middle of the night. She stood before him when Leon pulled the blindfold from his head.

All Niagara Falls then. Begged for his life.

In the end, they made a deal: He could keep breathing Iowa air if he signed the business over to her. She'd be a silent partner, of course, and earn a percentage, but the real perk would be to 'burrow' cars off the lot as she saw fit. Sometimes they'd leave the lot and never come back. Other times they'd show up a week later with 4,000 miles added to the odometer. Other times a completely different car turned up in its place. Mostly it balanced out. When it didn't, Jimbo Jamboree kept his mouth shut. Even with this deal, ole JJ didn't spend a lot of face time with her.

She and Carlos arrived at the lot about a quarter to close. Jimbo, after hiding in his office for fifteen minutes, tore outta the place promptly at five. One of his employees was still giving a hard sell to a newly-wed couple. By five-thirty, the place was empty.

Esmeralda, dressed in a pinstripe mini-skirt suit, strut the length of the closed showroom, the gentle clap of her heels hitting the polished floor. She walked between the muscle cars, dragging her fingers along their sides, and peered out the showroom window walls toward the rows of cars in the lot. She watched the faded multi-colored pennant streamers bob in the wind. She stood there for several minutes, and then marched over to the counter to grab her purse. She retrieved her cell from a smaller side pouch and hit speed dial as she put it to her ear.

Leon Hutchins stood slightly off balance out in a

field when the call came in, firing shots at glass bottle and aluminum can targets some thirty yards away. Echoes warbled out in all directions, passing through him (he seriously felt it, for sure) and caused a group of birds to flee a thicket into the sky. For a moment, he felt a tad dizzy, like he was up there with them.

The phone rang again from the passenger's seat. He ambled back to the car, wiped his mouth on the back of his hand, and flopped into the driver's seat. He inspected the phone, rubbed his temple.

Queenie.

"Leon," she said.

He didn't even realize he answered the call.

He tried to hone in on where the fuck he was, exactly. He was starting to freak out a bit (no shame there, champ) when she said his name a second time. Then it came back a bit.

"Answer the phone when I call," she said. "I've called half a dozen times since you took off with the—"

"Well, I'm sorry, love. I've been a bit busy here. All the crew is dead. Even the little abortion."

"I'm beginning to think you . . . The stuff's okay, though—right?"

"Ummmm—"

"I'm tryin' to remain patient with you—" There was venom building in that beautiful throat.

"What am I supposed to do here—huh? Throw me a fuckin' bone."

"Keep talkin' like that and I'm gonna cut out your tongue. You've got til tomorrow. Then me and Carlos come to collect."

The line went dead.

156

His right eyebrow shot up, sweat bolted from what was left of his hairline, and his irises went all googly for a second before zooming in on the phone again.

A couple thoughts were grave enough to predominate the rest of the white noise in his noddle.

Firstly, she knew. He heard it in her voice that *she* heard it in his voice. Leon was now certain Esmeralda had sussed out his plan from the night he left the compound.

Secondly, Leon was now certain he was a dead man.

After William and Sara returned to the house, Lionel escorted her to the bathroom tub and washed the mud from her feet.

In the kitchen, William raided the cupboards and found a couple cans of chicken noodle soup. He dumped them in a pot and put it on the stove. While it warmed he threw together some grilled cheese.

When his parents came in from the bathroom, he sat them down at the table and served the food. Since entering the house, Sara had been lucid—though she couldn't remember her journey to the creek—but withdrawn, perhaps tired. Lionel tried to engage her throughout the meal. She only responded with subtle shrugs, eyes focused on her bowl as she sipped at her spoon. William forced himself to eat a sandwich.

Sara stayed at the table when they had finished eating, and watched William wash the dishes in the sink. When he was done, she said she was tired. He helped her to her room and tucked her in bed. He left the door cracked and ventured from room to room in the quiet house looking for Lionel. He found him outside on the front steps.

William sat beside him, lighting a cigarette. They sat looking out into the yard. After a few minutes, William finally said, "We need to think about another situation." His voice seemed unintentionally loud in the silence.

Lionel didn't respond.

"It'd be a helluvah a lot safer. You could visit her every day."

Lionel continued to look out over the yard like his son hadn't spoken. Then, abruptly, he stood up and went back into the house.

Out in the yard, what remained of light threw a grayish blue over everything.

Leon turned from the frontage road onto the empty parking lot. The Charger's headlights cut a band out of the night that exposed the pink and black business sign. The joint was a slab of concrete ugliness that matched the sign, X's & O's in hot pink neon cursive over the entrance. Toward the back of the lot, a single light post flickered over a dumpster. Toothless Romeo's dogshit Caddie sat at the edge of the property. Beyond it, miles of nothing but dark hills. Leon gunned it to the front doors, gravel jangling in the wheel wells. He slammed the break, forearmed the car into park. He cranked the handle—throwing his knee and shoulder into it—and sprung from the car without bothering to close the door behind him.

A hand-written sign on the door read: CLOSED FOR RENOVATION. THE GIRLS OF X'S & O'S WILL RETURN. Leon yanked the door handle.

Pffft. Locked.

He spun around and legged it back to the car, grunted as he leaned down from the driver's seat, and patted the floor under the passenger's side until his fingers found the hatchet. Then, back at the entrance, he swung the tool, and the butt connected hard with the glass and shattered.

He dug for a handkerchief, wiped the handle, and reached an arm inside to unlock the door.

A little after nine William took a stool at the Rock Bottom. Some of the after work flies were beginning to filter out, but the place still buzzed with revelry. Two Mexicans, dressed like tejones, occupied a booth in the back. One of them, long-haired and gold-toothed, laughed as his companion finished a story, and they clanked their pints together. William was unsure about the western garb, but he could really get behind the gold tooth, thought someday maybe he'd get one on his right canine.

Over at the juke, two mechanics—both wore grease-stained blue shirts with name patches—punched in two selections and were weighing options on the third. A group of women had gathered around a pitcher at one of the tables, their conversation work-related but their eyes set on three younger studs pitching darts near the entrance. The mating ritual had begun. One of the women had quietly absconded to the bathroom only to

159

re-emerge with the top two buttons of her blouse undone. Only a matter of time before the two groups merged into one. He gave it forty minutes until the girls migrated to the vacant dartboard, pretending they couldn't wrap their heads around this Cricket thing. Inevitably, they'd call upon the meat men for assistance, and then the men, who had been posing and casually flexing their bare arms all night, would oblige to lend a hand.

Puke.

He turned back to the bar where the old timers and the incinerated hearts club slouched over their drinks and stared silently at some sporting event or reality television show that sucked all meaning from the world.

Oh, boy. Ugly one coming on.

This crowd already had a half a shift on him, and William was determined to catch up as quickly as possible.

"Well, I musta made some impression to get you back here," Delilah said, seeming to appear from some dark corner behind the bar.

"Nice place. Crown and Brown. Keep em comin'."

"Gonna need a card to open a tab, Detective—"

"Just William." He handed her his credit card.

When she returned with his drink, she said, "You ever find out who that poor girl was?"

"Working on it." He dropped his eyes and looked down the bar. The question jostled him from a head full of Wolfe farm absorption. He rooted out his notepad from his jacket, turned to the phone number he'd copied off the paper scrap from Rosemary's car.

He stood up and jingled his drink above his head. Delilah turned with raised eyebrows.

"Glass outside?"

"You should know the answer to that, hon."

"Right." He drained the drink and put the glass on the bar.

"Keep em coming," she said.

"Delilah, you are wonderful. Let's elope to Vegas."

Apparently, she'd heard this one before. She smiled anyway. Enough for a glimpse at her wrecked teeth. "Don't think my Ray would be wild about the idea."

He shook his head. "Heartbreaker."

Out in the alley, William lit up and dialed the number from the notepad. It rang seven times and then went to voicemail.

A pre-recorded message from a nebulous female said, "Thank you for calling X's and O's. We're currently undergoing a complete remodel of our lounge room. We apologize for the inconvenience. Reopening date to come. Email us at info at x, s, n, o, s, dot com. And if you're interested in becoming an X O girl, call—" William scrawled down the second number in his notepad. "Before contacting us, please remember you must be eighteen to be considered. Kisses."

He ended the call, dialed the number. Ten rings. No answer. No voicemail.

Back inside, William passed a figure in black sitting in the stool closest to the exit. He returned to his place to find a fresh drink waiting for him. He took a sip and sat down. When he looked up, he realized the figure was Roland.

Leon tore up the small set of stairs into the lounge. He boosted himself up onto the bar, leaned over and grabbed a Vodka bottle, unscrewed the cap, and chugged deeply. Marching further into the room, he took in his reflection on the dozens of mirrored walls. Each held a different contorted version of himself. His mind whirled at the fun house effect. Then his image dissolved and the mirrors went black, and he, too, thought he might pass out. Panic seized his lungs and he struggled to breathe and he suddenly knew everything was futile. He could rage and fight against it, but nothing he could do, no escape plan he could make, would reverse his decision and free him from wrath now.

Queen Bitch was coming.

He screamed and launched the Vodka toward the main stage. The bottle flew across the room—booze trailing its fabulous arch—and shattered against the wall behind the stage. The mirror there cracked in two, and the top half crashed to the floor in one giant sliver. He stomped forward across the room, growling in an attempt to shake free his unease, and kicked open the door at the back of the room.

It opened to a narrow hallway. Cinder block walls painted pink ended three yards down at an exit door. The real action happened here. He zipped past the VIP room and the two dressing rooms. Toothless Romeo's office was on the right. Moaning came from behind the door. Leon blew into the room. From behind his desk, a young stripper rode Toothless Romeo. She screamed and bounced off the fat fuck, covering her breasts with her arms. He flaunted a shocked smile. His nickname wasn't ironic—most of his top teeth were missing.

"So sorry to interrupt the casting session. I need a word. Quick, like."

Sweat ran from Toothless Romeo's balding hairline down past his cheek. Bush league beaver salesman.

"Leon, glad you dropped by. How bout you put that thing down and pop a squat."

Leon swung the hatchet into the desk. "Where is it?"

Toothless Romeo threw his hands up, each of his fat fingers ringed in gold. Leon could see him uselessly searching his noggin for a way out.

"I'm tired here, Vern. Been workin' long hours. Haven't slept for days. The ole boss is a real ball buster, so let's cut the bullshit." He wiped sweat at his temple like a preacher mid-sermon. "I been up and down the county and word is that mouthbreather down tucky way off'ed Georgie Boy and Frank. But you knew that, didn't you piggy."

Leon's pupils dilated, his breath heavy. He brandished a pistol from his jacket. The stripper, who had been cowering in the corner, gasped and began to cry.

"Where's my shit?"

"I don't have it. Leon, you look exhausted. Let's sit down and talk about this."

Leon pulled the trigger twice. The stripper fell into the corner, chin dropping to her chest.

"Oh, Jesus." Toothless Romeo's hands trembled. Sweat pooled under his chin and beneath his gold

163

necklace.

Leon moved around the desk, ripped open the drawer.

"I didn't know it was yours. Honest, man. Please."

Leon plucked out a fat bag. He remained silent as he dropped the bag onto the desktop. Pinched a sample and snorted it from his fingers. "This is definitely the new shit."

"I didn't know."

"Who you get this from then? Tucky Fuck's partners?"

"Some regulars threw it my way last night. Called and said they had some shit. Stopped by and gave me a sample. Said there was more if I wanted quantity. I'm not lying. I didn't know where it came from. Didn't ask, honestly."

Leon backhanded him across the face. "Gluttonous pig."

He scooped the bag into his jacket. The wheels turned. His eyes twitched. Then Leon unloaded a round into Toothless Romeo's knee cap. The fat man cried out and grabbed at the wound.

"It was Robert," he shouted.

Leon shot him twice in the chest.

19

"Put his drinks on my tab," William told Delilah when she set a shot and beer in front of Roland.

Since his return to the bar, William and his old friend had spent several minutes in uncomfortable silence. Roland, face obscured by his hoodie, had sat navel-gazing and twitching occasionally. William stared blankly at a TV and re-surveyed the bar. The group of women had already managed to merge with the dartboard studs. Twenty minutes early.

"Thanks," Roland said.

Delilah shrugged and backtracked to the other end of the bar.

"So I came across The Occupants' record," William started.

Roland nodded. "Which one?"

"I think it was called *Shaky Hands*?"

"Oh, yeah. That one—we recorded—cut that one—it was the last one we did. Recorded it up in Hegemony. Over at a buddy's—a friend's—studio—basement. Virtually killed the band."

"How so?"

Roland shrugged. "Dunno. Typical—the usual

band bullshit. Egos. Creative differences. And Walrus—
bass player—could hardly—he couldn't—he had to do,
like, forty takes."

"Walrus? That dude that was always whippin' his
dick out in high school?"

Roland laughed. "Yeah."

"I didn't know he even played an instrument."

"He didn't."

They both laughed.

"So should I listen to it or burn it?"

"I thought—there's a lot of cool stuff—tunes on
it. Kinda movin' away from typical—you know, your
normal—hardcore four piece. More diverse. I even did
some vocals—some singin' on a few tracks."

William smiled. "Nice. I'll definitely check it out."

"Where'd you—who gave you that?"

William winced a little. "I found it with some of
Rosemary's records."

"Really?" Roland took a drink.

The conversation petered out and William went
back to staring at the TV. After a few minutes, Roland
finally said, "You know—I'm sorry to hear—someone
told me about your mom. I always loved—Sara was—she
was always good to me."

"Thanks. I appreciate it. She did think the world
of you." William drained his drink, shaking the ice in his
glass as he set it on the bar. "Well, I gotta take a piss, then
I should get outta here."

"Yeah—I should—I gotta take off too."

"I'll give you a lift."

"Nah, that's—"

"Great. Hold tight." William slid from his stool

166

and maneuvered around the tables to the hallway leading to the bathroom.

Latching the hook on the bathroom door, William dipped into his special pocket and retrieved the tweak he filched from Rosemary's car. He wiped off the top of the urinal with a paper towel and tapped out a bump. He quickly snorted it, feeling the familiar burn at the back of his nasal passage. At the sink, he washed his hands, ran his wet palms through his hair a few times. He unlocked and opened the door, surprised to see a small line outside. He nodded to the gold-toothed tejone and one of dartboard studs as he cruised past them back toward the bar.

Toothless Romeo reeled out of a black vortex coughing up blood and came to in his chair. He looked over at Shelby in the corner. Blonde hair covered her face. Blood pooled at her naked thighs. He scanned the office, still dizzy, and saw the asshole had ransacked the place. His eyes shot to the filing cabinet at his left. The drawers were open, papers dumped on the floor.

He struggled to pull up his pants, and then stood slowly. Wheezing, he edged over to the cabinet, using the table for balance. Then, bracing himself against the wall, he pushed the cabinet aside. It took a few tries—he had no strength—but he managed to move the cabinet a few feet to the right enough to reach into the hole. He yanked the duffle bags out of the wall one at a time and slung them crisscross over his shoulders. He didn't remember them being as heavy when Robert's crew brought them over two nights before, and he thought he might fall over as he lumbered for the door. Darkness was at the edge of his vision and he felt lightheaded. He rested in the door jamb for a few minutes—his head buried in the crook of his arm—and he thought maybe he'd just sit down, wait for them to return.

But something about that wasn't right.

He opened his eyes and glanced at his shirt. Awful lotta blood. He needed to drive. Somewhere. He knew the place, just couldn't think of the word.

Then he was moving again, supporting himself against the concrete—cool on his shoulder—as he staggered down the pink hallway to the exit door. He pushed it open enough to stumble outside.

The air felt good on his cheeks. Even better than the concrete. He was so hot. He zigzagged toward his car, gravel crunching beneath his feet. The sound was so loud.

At the driver's side, he rummaged in his pocket for his keys, but he became dizzy again and fell over. He examined his hands and they were raw from the gravel but he couldn't feel anything. He got to his knees and reached up from his place on the ground and unlocked the door. Then he used the side of the car to help him to his feet. He opened the door and flopped in behind the wheel. Turned the key in the ignition.

He was tired now. Wanted to rest again. He struggled to shift the car into drive. And then he was moving forward. Into the dark field. Away from X's & O's. Needed to go the other way. To the road. The song on the radio—he always liked it.

Then the black vortex came again and he closed his eyes.

William settled in and started the car, unlocked the door for Roland. Roland eased into the seat like he was an eighty-year-old man with hemorrhoid flare up.

"Let's go gramps."

"Yeah. Yeah." Roland swung the door closed, cocking his head to the speakers.

"A person without roots must be sick, must die. They become something like a hungry ghost. So many have left everything behind, wandering around like a hungry ghost. Searching for something to belong to, something to believe in. You look at the way they walk. The loneliness can be felt. They don't look like regular human beings. Because they are hungry ghosts. They are very hungry for love, for understanding—"

"What are you—the fuck is this?"

William laughed, pulled away from the curb. "A dharma talk."

"A dhar—what?" Roland laughed. "This some new age shit, right?"

"More like old age shit, but—yeah."

"I mean, what'd they do—what happened to you in the big city. Jesus. A hippie cop? That doesn't even make—that's ridiculous."

"Yeah. Yeah."

"Please don't tell me we have to—I'm not gonna listen to this all the way there. I'll get out and walk."

William turned on the overhead. "Nah, have at it."

Roland ejected the disc and then rifled through the CDs at his feet. He looked up. "Donovan?"

"Shut up," William said playfully.

169

Roland popped in *South of Heaven.*

William slowed as they neared a stop sign. No other cars. He idled for a moment, drumming the wheel with his thumbs, and turned to Roland with a devilish grin. "Know what we should do?"

"No idea."

"Woodridge Road."

"No way."

"We're doing it."

"You're a cop."

"And?"

"It's stupid."

"And?"

"We're gonna die."

"Nice night for it."

William hesitated. Then suddenly reassured, he flipped the turn signal, and accelerated right onto Fredrickson Ave.

Music burst out the windows the entire ten minutes to Woodridge. After turning onto the darkened road, William pulled to the shoulder. His heart thundered in his chest. Sweat under arms.

He shut off the music.

"Let's do it, then," Roland said, his voice calm.

William steered back onto the road. In the headlights, dying rows of cornfields walled both sides of the one lane blacktop. He killed the headlights. The road and the corn went black.

He stomped on the gas. The car shot forward. He tightened his grip on the wheel and tightened his arms. The car picked up speed, and the speedometer shot up. His heart followed it. William gritted his teeth, eyes

170

focused on the horizon. All he could hear was the wind.

His heart was threatening to cannonball from his chest out the windshield, and then . . . they were airborne.

The small drop was only a few feet but it seemed like seconds before the back of the car collided with the blacktop. A horrible scratching sound followed, and in the side mirror William caught orange sparks in the black. They lurched forward, seatbelts tightened around their chest, and then, as the car careened uphill, they were thrown back into the seats.

They sped up the seven foot incline and shot into the air again. Time slowed. Then they bottomed out for a second time, the force of the crash tossing them up from their seats. Roland's arms flopped about. William's jaw slammed together. He hit the break. His hands bounced from the wheel. The car screeched to a jerky stop.

They didn't speak.

William lit a smoke, took a drag, and handed it to Roland.

"Again?" William asked, flipping on the headlights.

"Good to go, if you are."

But William turned the car around and headed toward Black River. Roland didn't switch on the music. Instead, they traveled in silence, passing the cigarette back and forth, and let the wind blow in, loud and violent. Like a hungry ghost.

William stopped in front of Sheryl's house, and threw the car into park. Roland took a final drag off another cigarette and flicked it out the window.

"You're still one crazy motherfucker," he said.

"Says the man who blew himself up."

"Maybe next we go fishing."

"Deal."

Roland pushed opened the door, lifted his right leg out onto the brick road, and then he paused, looking at William. "I ain't judging, Willie, but I could see it—I saw it in your eyes—the first time you came here."

"What are you talking about?"

"Right." Roland climbed out of the car and shut the door. William watched his old friend struggle up the driveway and into the house. He turned on the overhead and searched for the dharma talk CD. When he located it, he ejected the Slayer album, and slid it in before pulling away from the curb.

William was on his third Crown and Brown, finally feeling himself for the first time all day, when a man with a pencil mustache and a brown Members Only jacket paraded into the bar with his pregnant girlfriend. After dropping Roland off, he'd promised himself he'd stop for one. Famous last words. One flowed into two, two into three. He opted for somewhere new—Plumpie's or Pukie's or something. He was the sole customer for the first hour.

The couple ordered a pitcher and a half hour later, they were laughing and hollering at the juke. An old jump blues crackled from the speakers and the two broke out into a peculiar hobo kind of boogie woogie. The woman waddled about as best she could. The man danced out of time, a graceless madman off his meds.

172

When the song finished, William hopped from his stool and clapped.

"Bravo!" he hollered.

"Thanks, slick," said the man. "That's our song."

William cut the volume on the mediation CD. It was eleven fifty seven according to the dashboard clock and in front of him the corroded 1980's landyacht eased down Hillview Mobile Home Lodge, gravel grumbling under its wheels, knotted branches stretched out above him from shadows between trailers.

The landyacht parked in the drive at the end of a small cul de sac, hisses and clinks caroming from somewhere inside its geriatric intestines. William's new friends, Francine and Bruce, stumbled out of the car. He parked behind them, the back end of his car hanging out the driveway into the street. As he walked up the drive to join them, what he initially believed to be ivy creeping up the trailer's sides was actually military grade camo netting.

"It come like that?" William jabbed a thumb at the trailer, following the couple to cracked concrete steps.

"All me, slick," Bruce said out the side of his mouth, unlocking the door.

In the kitchen, Francine boiled a kettle of water. Bruce had disappeared from the room for a few minutes and re-emerged with a mint tin and a small mirror. He straddled a chair at the kitchen table and opened the little tin and took out a bindle and ever-so-carefully tapped the contents on to the mirror and pinched a razor from the tin and tapped it lightly on the mirror, clicking his tongue against the roof of his mouth as he panned the room, a smile on one side of his mouth. He cut some lines and snorted one and then handed the rolled-up dollar bill to William.

William arched to the mirror and Bruce hopped up from the table and went to the living room. William saw him turn on an old radio. Low static filled the trailer. Bruce moved from view, but William could hear him rummage through the corner.

Francine's kettle whistled and she rose to grab it from the stove and returned to the table. She poured the hot water into a mug in front of William, topping it off with a dash from a flask. She winked at William, and poured both the hot water and whatever was in the flask into her own mug.

He bobbed the teabag and sipped from the mug.

"Bruce, you comin' back or what?" she hollered, craning her neck toward the doorway.

She eased back into her chair then she took a snort for herself.

William tapped out a tense rhythm on the countertop. His knees bounced underneath it. Thoughts tore down the highway of his mind—none of them good. He had the violent urge to leave, to claw at the nicotine-stained curtains, to crawl out the window back into the night. The skin stretched too tightly across his bones— the bones too tight for the marrow. None of it was right. None of it was him.

Francine stood, hands at her lower back, and shuffled to the kitchen archway.

"Bruce, you want 'nother or what?" she asked.

Bruce sat cross-legged on the floor, sweating over a pile of screws next an old coffee can. He sifted through the pile, occasionally picking one from the others to examine it and then meticulously arrange it at the bottom of the coffee can.

"Bruce," Francine repeated.

No answer. He continued his task as if she hadn't spoken at all. Bruce's world was only the screws and coffee can now.

"He's at those screws again. Never met a man so particular about his things." She motioned to the table. "Go ahead—he'll be there for awhile."

William shook his head.

"Third time at those things this week." Francine lit a cigarette and grimaced into her seat. "Can't wait til this lil guy gets here. Killin' my back." She scooted the mirror toward her and inhaled a line. She sniffed, "But I don't know what we're gonna do about that doctor. We were there last month. You know what he says to me? The doctor."

William's face twitched, covered in sweat.

"The idiot does his proddin' and pokin' and says, he says, my baby died. Dead inside me. Now how's that gonna be? You ever heard such nonsense in your life? I mean, how's he gonna tell me that? How's he gonna tell a mother such things? What does he know, anyway? They let anybody be a anything these days. I mean, I'm the mother for god sakes."

William glanced down at her belly and flashed on the image of Francine's baby suspended in brackish amniotic fluid, limbs slack and inert, flesh the color and condition of a channel cat's belly.

He wondered if they'd sit at this table and eat the placenta. After it was born. Or passed or whatever.

175

She sniffed again. "I think I'd know a little better'n him. I'd feel it if there was something wrong, ya know?" Francine rubbed her belly in gentle circles with both hands. "Huh, baby? Yeah, I love you. Yes, I do."

"Did you wanna feel 'im?" She asked.

Without waiting for a reply, she reached across the table and pulled his hand to her belly.

"The fuck's goin' on in there?" Bruce shouted from the other room, hovered over his pile of screws. "You tryin' fuck my lady? I'm in the next goddamn room. I can hear every word you're sayin', slick. Every goddamn word."

William raced the back roads outside Black River, window rolled down to let the cool night air in. He had been traveling from one darkened stretch to the next since leaving Bruce and Francine's.

The longer he drove, the more erratic his driving became. Turning at a three way stop, he ran the sign and swerved into the shoulder, side-swiping a row of bushes. He corrected the vehicle before it ran completely off the road. The back wheels threw up a protest of gravel.

He continued on for another three miles, gaining speed. As he neared a hill, he reached over for his cigarette pack on the passenger seat. He looked up to see a dog in the middle of the road—its blue eyes locked on his. Then he gasped and jerked the wheel to the right, but it was too late, and he felt and heard the impact of the dog against the left fender. The car veered off the road, crashed into a wobbly split rail, and bucked against uneven mounds in an empty field until it collided with something in the dark.

William shot forward into the airbag.

When he came to he was already on his feet moving away from the car. He looked back over his shoulder at the dented fender. An ailed clicking sound echoed from the engine. He turned away and stumbled in the dirt. Up ahead, he could see firelight. He moved toward it. The field was quiet except for the clicking engine, which didn't recede even after he ventured too far away to see the car.

William closed in on the firelight. A crowd of men had gathered in a circle, and fires spewed forth from rusted barrels. The men hollered and cheered, but he could hear growling beneath their voices. They slapped each other across the back with fistfuls of money. Their mouths tiny black holes framed with yellow teeth.

He pushed his way into the circle.

In bright orange and yellow light, two bloody dogs, saliva at their fangs, sprang toward each other. A chunk of flesh opened at the black dog's torso. The other clawed at the jowls. Their muscular haunches and paws struggled for balance in the dirt. Then the black dog overpowered the other and drove it to the ground. It snarled, waiting for the right moment to strike.

William retreated from the circle and walked into the tall grass beyond the men. He came to a ditch and climbed it to a road. There, in the middle of the road, his son stood holding a red ball. William ran to the boy, but the boy backed away and pointed down the road. Ambling in that direction, William saw a dog lying on its side. He approached, unsure if it was still alive, but as he got closer, there was a visible undulation at its belly.

"Goddammit," William sighed, kneeling to the dog.

The dog looked up at him with fear in its eyes.

A memory rushed to the forefront of his mind—one he had forgotten since he was a boy. When William was seven he had been playing outside the barn. A whimper from the field behind drew him from his play world. He stood and listened for a short time, and then hopped the fence and drudged into the grass. He followed the cries to the glade. A stray dog writhed under a tree. It was bleeding from its withers. He advanced with hesitation. Blood pooled beneath it, mixed with grass and helicopter maple seeds. Standing there, he felt dazed and powerless.

William ran back to the house.

"Mom! Dad!" he cried as he reached the backdoor.

Lionel came to the screen. "Why you yellin'?"

"A dog—it's hurt over there at the edge of the woods."

"What'd we tell you about goin' out there on your own?"

"I know but . . . it's sad cause it's bleeding. I heard him crying." Tears ran down William's cheeks. "I don't like that noise. Help him, dad."

As William finished, Sara came to the door.

"What's going on?" She asked.

"He found an injured dog out past the fence there."

Lionel stormed up the stairs and emerged from

178

the house a few minutes later carrying his rifle. Sara followed him out. Lionel continued toward the fence.

"No, Dad! We gotta help it. We gotta save it." William was sobbing now and ran to his mother.

"Lionel," Sara said.

Lionel stopped mid-stride, sighed, and turned back. He squatted down to William's eye level. "I'm gonna go check it out. If, as you say, that thing is hurt bad and it's beyond saving, then the most merciful thing to do is to put it out of its misery."

Then Lionel rose and marched to the glade.

Later, at the dinner table, the three of them sat in silence. William hadn't touched his food.

"You need to eat your food," Lionel said.

"I'm not hungry."

Lionel shot a pleading look at Sara.

"Why are you mad at your father?"

"He didn't have to kill it."

Lionel set his fork down and wiped his hand on a napkin. "I know it isn't fair. A lot of times, that's just how it is. It's hard to wrap your mind around the world." He paused. "That's never gonna change no matter how old you are. It's always gonna be bigger and meaner than you'll be able to understand."

He put a hand on William's head.

"The only kind of help we could offer was to end its suffering as quickly and painlessly as possible," Sara said, embracing William.

Coming back to the present, William leaned forward and reached a hand toward the dog. It managed a growl. Wiping blood from his lip, he pulled his gun.

Then he stood up and fired a single shot into the

dog.

William opened his eyes. Light had just broken the horizon line at the edge of the field. A deflated airbag hung from the steering wheel. He groaned and adjusted the rearview so he could see his face. Dried blood at his lips.

He threw an elbow over the seat and looked through the rear windshield. He was about eighty yards from the road.

He started the car and put it in reverse.

After several attempts, he was able to free the wheels from the dirt mound, and he drove in reverse to the road. Hitting gravel, he corrected the vehicle, and before putting it in drive, William sighed and lit a cigarette.

He retraced his journey from the night before, but nowhere on the road was a dead dog.

20

The mid-day sun blasted a tawny cornfield in white, outside Leon's window. He grimaced and grasped the sunglasses draped over his shirt. He slid them on, checked his look in the rearview. Grinned at his reflection, ticked his tongue off the roof of his mouth. Handsome demon.

Tendrils on the ground had informed him Robert Crimley was a local loser who fancied himself some kind of survivalist guru with a small crew of flunkies set on a hostile takeover. Same ears had tipped him to Tucky Fuck. At the time, douche bag had run his mouth about the hit on the Grass brothers. Lone gunman. But, apparently, Oswald hadn't acted alone. Leon shoulda known. Mouthbreather couldn't set up a game of checkers without someone telling him where to place the pieces. Robert Crimley and his crew were the shadowy force on the grassy knoll. And their rat, Toothless Romeo.

He cruised down the blacktop, his knuckles white around the wheel. He glanced into the rearview again. A motorcycle was burning rubber fifty yards back.

Everything was coming to light under the Iowa sun, and Leon would deal with Robert the same way he dealt with the first two. Then, after he had the goods, maybe he'd make his way somewhere with better weather. Florida. Vegas. Acapulco.

His eyes drifted back to the rearview. The motorcycle had veered into the opposite lane, gaining speed to pass. A few seconds later, it disappeared into his blind spot. This guy was some asshole.

Leon could sense the rider outside his window. Instead of continuing on and passing him, Leon could still feel him there maintaining equal speed. He looked over to give the guy a what-the-fuck. The rider wore black leather and a helmet. Leon saw himself in the mirrored face shield.

Then, keeping his left hand on the handle bar, the rider reached into his black leather and pulled a semi-automatic.

Leon instinctively stomped the break. The Charger squealed.

The rider unloaded a spurt of fire that shattered the window and tore holes in the fender. Glass exploded into the car, but the bullets missed Leon. The Charger stopped, fishtailing slightly. He jerked over to the AK-47 on the passenger's seat. Returned fire into the rider. The rider fell back, the bike dropped.

Leon cuddled his gun, breath heavy, in a daze. He was still processing the attack when he glanced up into the rearview in time to see a van slam into him. His head bounced off the steering wheel.

"Move it, move it, move it. Let's go," a voice yelled from behind.

Four figures, all covered by ski masks, vaulted from the van and hurried toward the car. Leon pawed for his weapon. It wasn't there. The force of the collision had knocked it to the floor of the passenger's seat. As he lunged for it, two of the men ripped open the door and dragged him from the car.

He threw a blind punch that landed on one of their jaws, but soon all four men had him on the pavement pummeling him with punches and kicks. Two of them frantically zip tied his hands. Another tossed a bag over his head and Leon's sight went black.

William had stopped by his place to clean up before heading into work. After a quick shower, he had decided to run a razor over his week-old stubble. He brushed his teeth and combed his hair. He didn't feel like a new man, but he looked like one.

As the station's automatic doors slid open, his heart revved and he felt something like terror pass over him. He tried to hurry through the front office area, but Widy and Darwin Cash were at their cubicles, downing coffee and shooting the shit. Seeing William, Widy grinned, showing off his sizeable buck teeth, and hollered, "Well, well, lookin' good, Mr. Handsome!"

William nodded, and stood there politely while Widy went into his usual stories. At a certain point, it was like somebody turned the volume down on him. William could see the man's mouth moving, but he couldn't hear words coming out. He just smiled and continued to nod. Meanwhile, an emotional tidal wave was rising somewhere inside William.

Once there was a lull in Widy's chronicles, William excused himself and dashed away to his office. He shut the door and settled into his chair, sweat staining his shirt. His eyes fell to the picture of his son next to the computer monitor.

He searched his pockets and found his phone. Culled his contacts. Angie was the first number. He tapped the screen.

It rang.

Changing his mind, he ended the call.

William dropped his head to the desk, closed his eyes, and began to weep.

William had received the same message when he tried to call the number for X's & O's. And, again, there was no answer on the second line.

Needing fresh air, and wanting to get away from the station, he drove out to the club.

He could see from the car that the front door had been broken, and he drew his gun before stepping outside. Loose shards of glass cracked beneath his feet at the front door as he moved into the strip joint.

Ascending the small set of stairs, he advanced into the main lounge at a slight crouch. The room was dark, full of mirrors, tables, and various dancing stations with poles. At the main stage, fragments from a fractured wall mirror lay scattered about on the floor. A broken bottle of vodka lay among the rubble. William glided to a door next to the stage. He nudged it open, leading with his gun.

He eased into a pink hallway. A low drone of

florescent lights filled the area. Further down, a trail of blood spatter lead from a door on the right to the back exit. He stepped to the room, an office, and saw a dead naked girl recoiled in the corner, two gunshot wounds to the chest.

The room had been ravaged. A coffee table overturned. Papers from a filing cabinet strewn all over the floor. Coats, still on hangers, flung from a small closet. Blood lead across the shag carpet and disappeared around a desk. The contents of the desk drawers emptied and piled on the floor. William followed it. More blood there at the chair.

He noticed, then, a hole in the wall next to the filing cabinet. Looked like someone simply took a hammer to the drywall. He traipsed to the wall, hung an arm into the hole. Fairly large area. He surveyed the room again, scratching his cheek with his shoulder. Then he returned to the pink hallway, tracked the blood splatter to the exit.

Outside the sun was bright.

He walked a few yards toward the dumpster, cupping a hand over his temple to shade his eyes from the sun. After some examination, he found a small amount of blood in the gravel. He knelt down, studied the parking lot for a moment. He sighed. Then, for some reason, he gazed out into the field beyond the dumpster. That's when he saw it—the car. A green Caddie. The driver's side door was open. He'd missed it on the way in. It was clearly visible from the lot entrance.

He waded out into the thick brown overgrowth. As he closed the gap, he could make out a figure at the wheel. A bloody hand, fat fingers ringed in gold, dangled from the door.

No more than five feet five inches, the man was heavy and dressed in a cheap suit. His limp head had fallen back. Flies danced around his bald scalp. He'd slung two duffle bags around his bloody chest. Explained why he couldn't get the door shut. When William reached the door, he stared in at the man for a moment, and then rifled through his pockets. He found a money clip of hundreds. A black and pink business card read:

Romeo Scalanti
X's & O's owner

William put the money clip back into the dead man's jacket, pocketed the business card. He unzipped the duffle bag, exposing the tightly packaged meth inside.

"Shit," William said to himself. Then to Romeo, he said, "Looks like your friends forgot something."

William paused, scrutinized the area. Then he lit a cigarette and fetched his phone from his jacket. When Addie answered, he said, "Gonna need assistance to X's & O's. Eight hundred Holiday Road. We got multiple homicides out here."

William could barely make out Lionel's silhouette on the steps when he pulled up the drive. He parked the car and walked around to the front of the house.

"Your mother disappeared again," Lionel said when William approached and asked him how things were going. It was too dark to make out his face, but William could tell Lionel was crying, could hear it in his voice. "I found her out on the road there, bout two miles down. Almost to the Davison property. Pulled the truck over to the shoulder. She didn't know who I was." His voice trembled. "She was afraid of me."

William put a hand on his father's shoulder.

"My wife of forty years, son. She can't see me anymore. Her eyes . . ." He trailed off.

"She's gone. The Sara we know is gone."

After sitting for some time with Lionel, William returned to the car. He unlocked the trunk. Then, lifting one at a time, he shouldered the two duffle bags and walked out into the dark toward the barn.

PART THREE

THE BIG COMEDOWN

21

Passing the Pump N Dump on the split sidewalk with a rod over his shoulder and a small plastic lure box jammed between his bicep and ribs, Roland hiked toward the river. Relatively warm, gray clouds obscured the early morning sun. He hadn't slept, spent the night recording, and after firing up the last of his shit, he got a wild hair up his ass to go fishing.

It'd been years. Before his father's heart attack, he and the old man would wake up at the ass crack of dawn every weekend and cruise the dark water looking for downed logs or weed lines where largemouth would hide in ambush. In the evenings, they would head to shore and build a fire from the driftwood. They'd put out bank lines rigged up with chunks of sunfish and wait for big flathead cat to swallow them whole. Over the years, they hauled up some monsters.

Roland remembered his father telling him there was at least a hundred and nineteen species of fish in the Black River, which seemed a bit of a tall tale. By himself, Roland rarely caught anything other than bluegill. Once, with his father's help, he did manage to reel in a twelve inch walleye. He could still see the prideful look on his old man's face. There was a snapshot of the small triumph in a drawer somewhere in his mother's house.

In high school, he and Willie and a few others would sometimes head out farther up the river, up into Carlson County. Mostly, it was an excuse to get out of dodge. They never caught much more than a buzz. They'd sit along the river listening to tunes from the car stereo, smoke pot, drink beer stolen from his mother's fridge. They wouldn't have known what to do with a fish if they'd caught one. William would never be able to unhook the fish anyway. He'd always had a soft spot for little creatures. Roland even had to put the worm on his hook. William said it made him feel bad.

Roland smiled at the memory as he crossed the highway and made his way into the grassy ditch. He walked a well-worn path up the small hill. At the top, he noticed some remnants of police tape snapping in the wind. His mood dropped suddenly—fresher memories replaced the older ones. He took a slow breath, surveying the river below, and descended the hill.

He stood at the river bank and cast a shallow running crankbait along the patches of green lily pads that remained among the newly brown and receded weed lines. He worked at the outside edges of the round pads––reeling steady and occasionally flicking his wrist to mimic a wounded minnow. He did this for some time without a strike. When the subtle vibration of the lure ceased on the retrieve, he reeled the line in and discovered long drooping weeds entangled in its hooks. He removed the nuisance and decided to move on to another spot. Bass often congregated in small bunches to feed in shade. Casting out under the bridge near the pilings might prove exciting. His face and back were beginning to hurt, but he decided to give it another hour.

He walked the trail at the river's edge, and as he got closer to the bridge, he noticed a small lump on the ground. It looked like a pile of dirty clothes, but after twenty more feet, he saw it was someone sleeping under a blanket. He tottered forward into the shadows beneath the bridge and hovered next to the body. He slouched down a bit and hesitated. Then, with the end of his rod, he poked the figure in the side.

Immediately, a boy threw back the blanket, letting out a terrified yelp, and crab-walked backwards toward the wall. It was the Mexican kid, the one he'd seen around the neighborhood all week.

"I didn't—I'm sorry to frighten you." The kid panted, his eyes focused on Roland like he was trying to acclimate to the waking world. "You don't have to be—I know I look fucked up, but I ain't gonna hurt—ain't gonna eat you."

The kid just looked at him for a moment, and then said, "Did you kill that girl?"

Roland squinted hard at the kid and twitched. "No, I didn't kill that girl."

"It's just I saw you. Sheriff came and got you."

"I knew her. She was my…" He trailed off.

"You did?"

Roland nodded and wiped at his lip. Glanced away from the kid. The sun had broken through the clouds.

"I found her. Or part of her. Down here." The kid motioned in the direction of where Roland had been fishing. "Right over there."

"Whaddya mean 'part of her?'"

"She was cut up. Someone chopped her into pieces. Sheriff didn't tell you that?"

Roland's vision swirled. He dropped to his ass. The kid said something but it sounded distant and warbled. He sat there.

At some point, the kid got up and left. Roland watched him walk off down the river. Then he let his mind drift into the sun's reflection on the water shattered into a million sparkling jewels.

Leon woke up when he heard the door open. His arms, tied behind him in the chair, had gone numb sometime in the night. The burlap sack obscured his vision (and itched like a bad case of scabies), but he could make out two figures enter the shed. The one in front hustled to him and removed the sack—a skinheaded Neanderthal, close to seven foot, built like he spent his days foraging for 'roids and whey protein shakes. Bad prison time Nazi ink covered his arms. Behind him stood a shorter man with his arms crossed over his belly. Flannel shirt. Mountain man beard. Their ensemble didn't gel.

"You fuckin' twits," Leon mumbled.

The bearded one nodded to the Neanderthal. "Floyd."

Floyd unleashed a blast to Leon's face.

194

Leon cackled as his head snapped back. He spit a glob of blood and snot toward the bearded one. Missed wide.

"I appreciate your candor, Leon. Shame you're such a lapdog for that spic cunt." The bearded one scratched his nose cocky-like. "Question is: How much you think she's gonna pay to get her nigger back?"

Clearly, he'd been practicing this little speech in the mirror. A smile broke the corner of Leon's bloody lips.

"You're holdin' me for ransom?! Funny shit, boys. Best you just let me go, head back to whatever cave you crawled out of. You're outta your depth here. Amateurs. Gonna get hurt."

Floyd rocked him with another shot to the face.

"You wanna call her or do you want me to?" Leon said as blood dripped from his nose. He looked at Floyd and said in all seriousness, "Phone's inside my jacket. Why don't you grab it and toss it to Paul Bunyan. Let's get this on. I got business elsewhere."

Floyd looked to the other for approval and, after he got it, he bent down and reached into Leon's jacket.

"Oopsy daisy—other side."

When Floyd moved for the other side of the jacket, Leon shifted his hips in the seat, threw his legs up and around the bigger man's torso, and pulled him in close. Then Leon sunk his teeth into Floyd's neck.

"He's biting me," Floyd screamed.

Floyd pushed against Leon's chest, and as he did Leon bit down harder. When that didn't free him, he unloaded a hook to Leon's stomach that caused Leon to relinquish his teeth. Leon spit out a piece of flesh. Blood

195

poured from Floyd's neck. He clutched the wound and twisted his body to the right, knocking Leon's chair to the floor as he freed himself.

The bearded one ran over and kicked Leon in the chest. Floyd staggered away, still clutching his neck.

The shed door burst open again and two more heavies barreled in. Leon peered up and smiled.

22

William sat at his desk and stared at the evidence from Rosemary's car. He was missing something. Something easy. Something right in front of him.

He massaged his temple—headache coming on. He got up and went to the coffee machine, and, returning to his office with a cup, he rooted out the Adderall bottle from his jacket pocket. Popped a capsule. Killed the coffee in two swallows. He slammed the empty cup on the desk.

In the top drawer, he located the Icy Hot bottle and smeared some of the balm on the back of his neck and under his eyes. He leaned back in the chair as the mentholated burn permeated his pores, working its way deep into his sinus cavity.

"You all right, sir?" a voice said with an accompanying knock on the open door.

William opened his eyes, wiped a tear away from his left cheek.

"Fine, Darwin. What's up?"

"Thought you might want this." Darwin Cash stepped into the room, holding out a cell phone. "Romeo Scalanti's. Found it under the desk in his office."

William took the phone.

"Looks like you could use about a week of sleep."

"I'm fine," William said again, but Darwin was already out the door.

He turned on the phone. A close-up snapshot of a girl's black and pink panties filled the screen. He scrolled the contacts. Over two hundred names and numbers. Mostly women. Anna. Candy. Esmeralda. Jaena. There were men's names too. Floyd. Harrison. Leon. One name caught his attention over the others.

Rosemary.

He set the phone down and turned back to the evidence on his desk. Something easy. Something right in front of him. He picked up the evidence bag of garbage, examined it for a moment and then tossed it aside. Then he picked up the bag of receipts. He opened it, and flipped through them. Then he flipped through them again. Bottled water. Cigarettes. Potato chips. Nothing unusual there. Same stuff everyone bought at a gas station.

It's when he was comparing the dates that he made the connection. At the bottom of every receipt was the same clerk's name.

Eugene.

"'Mary's mom is preparing the decorations for Mary's party on Saturday.'" Robert read, hunched over Carson's shoulder to see the worksheet on the kitchen table. "'She blew up six balloons in the morning and seven balloons in the afternoon. How many did she blow up for the party?'"

Robert eyed his son, tugging at the whiskers of his beard.

Carson looked back at him and sighed, "I know how to read it, dad. I don't know how to do it."

"What you talkin' about? This is a piece of cake. Baby stuff. You ain't a baby are you?"

Tonya looked up from the pot of chili on the stove. "Robert . . ." she said in a displeased tone.

"No, but I—" Carson dropped the pencil. "I hate word problems."

"Well, we're gonna have other problems if you don't pick that pencil back up."

Carson grabbed the pencil, and rested his head on his other hand.

Robert tapped his son's shoulder. "Look, read that last sentence again."

The boy re-read the sentence aloud.

"Good. That's the answer," Robert said, picking up his coffee mug and moving away from the table.

"What?! That's not the answer."

"The answer's there in that last question. What are they asking?"

"How many did she blow up."

"How many what?"

"Balloons."

"Right. So what's another way to say 'how many'?" He paused for a moment as if to let it sink in. "I've gotta step outside for a second, and when I come back I want you to have it solved."

"But it's supposed to be free time now," Carson whined.

"Then you better hurry up." Robert strode to Tonya and put a hand on her waist. "Hey, good lookin' whatcha got cookin'?" he sang.

"Nothin' for you."

Robert smiled and patted her on the ass. Then he turned and went out the door.

He took a drink from his mug and walked the length of the porch. With its peeling paint and grayed wood, the old Revival had seen better days. Running a hand along the porch rail might be an easy way to get splinter, but Robert liked weathered things and the house made him feel at ease. Tonya had other ideas. She wanted a total renovation. The money just hadn't been there for it.

But that was about to change.

King of his domain, he took another sip from his mug and absorbed the landscape. The sky was dry-brushed blue. Rolling hills of cornfields and copse spread out in front of the house for miles. He could make out Markus Thompson's silo in the distance. Sparrows played tunes nearby.

There wasn't anywhere else he'd rather live. This piece of land—it was about all a man could have of freedom these days. Away from the diseases of cities. Enough solitude from neighbors and the encroaching eye of government.

He took Leon's phone from the breast pocket of his flannel and located Esmeralda's number.

The glass door beeped as William entered the Pump N Dump.

A middle-aged clerk—bald on top with long stringy gray on the sides—gawked at him from behind the counter. When William approached, he noticed the clerk's finger nails were a half inch long, immaculately filed and cleaned. They made delicate clicks as he tapped them on the counter top. The man didn't say anything. He just stared at William. William stared back.

"Yeah?" the clerk said, raising his eyebrows.

"Man named Eugene work here?"

"Do I look like the manager?"

William moaned and flashed his badge. "Do I look like I have time for your shit?"

"It's a troublesome reality of our modern society that we are reminded of domestic violence on an almost daily basis. Unfortunately, even here in Hegemony we are not immune from this ugly truth." Janet Thurman, executive director of Safe House, paused before leaning closer to the podium mic. "Just last year Anna Hagaman was murdered in her home, while Anna's two children slept in the next room. Wendon Cook, the biological father of the children, was charged with the crime and is soon to stand trial.

"Since Safe House opened its doors in nineteen thirty-nine, it's been a haven for women and their children in similar situations as Anna Hagaman. The pressure on our shelters is getting greater and Safe House was in need of a massive renovation. As many of you may know, we received a grant from the Iowa Housing Finance Agency for two-thirds of the project cost contingent on our organization raising the additional

201

funds. What you may not know, however, is that the project was in dire need of finding that remaining funding until local business woman, Esmeralda Castillo, was kind enough to step up to the plate and donate the rest.

"Because of this, I have invited Ms. Castillo here today and would like her to have the honor of cutting the ribbon on our renovated shelter." Janet Thurman smiled and motioned to Esmeralda, who stood a few feet behind her. The small crowd applauded as Esmeralda accepted a pair of scissors from another official and stepped behind the pink ribbon.

She sheared the ribbon in one smooth motion. The crowd whistled and cheered. Stepping back to her place, Esmeralda felt her phone vibrate in her pocket. She pulled it out.

Leon.

"I'm very sorry, but I must take this," she said to those around her. Then she trotted inside the front doors of the Safe House. When she was certain the lobby was empty, she answered the call. "Solve your problems?"

"No, he hasn't, Ms. Castillo. Sadly, he's found more." The man's voice was throaty, full of hubris.

"Who is this?"

"Leon's babysitter."

"Right." She lowered her voice, remaining calm. "Do you know who the fuck I am?"

"Ah . . . yes. We're well aware of your . . . various business ventures. Quite the Rotary Club icon."

"What do you want?"

"An exchange."

"Of course. How much?"

"Two hundred fifty thousand."

For that kind of money, Leon should rot. Then again, she didn't want anyone else doing the dirty work. Not on this one.

"How do I know he's alive?"

"We wouldn't be talkin' otherwise."

"And I suppose you're behind these inconveniences in Black River."

"Things change, Ms. Castillo."

No—they didn't actually. It was always the same.

"Are you sure you want to do this?"

The man laughed.

"Give me two hours and I'll call you back."

Cutting Edge Hair Designs was a converted house on South Fredrickson, almost outside of town. Covered in dirty clapboard, the small salon had a hand-painted sign in the front window that listed business hours. William walked up the side driveway and climbed the rickety wooden staircase to a door.

He knocked.

"Who's there?" a voice called from inside.

"Mr. Standler, it's Detective William Wolfe. I need to speak with you."

It was quiet for a moment and then William heard the sound of a chain slacken. An imposing, unkempt man in his fifties answered the door.

The man smiled. "Come on in."

William stepped into the kitchen—a small cramped area with a low ceiling, longer than it was wide.

"And you're Mr. Standler?"

"Call me Eugene," the man said as he lead William into the next room.

A mattress was set against the far wall where the room sloped down at a sharp angle from the shape of the gable, Formica table and chair by a window near the entrance. Arranged neatly, almost methodically, vintage boxing posters hung on every wall.

William stopped at a framed black and white.

"That's me," Eugene said.

The picture was of a younger, leaner, Eugene Standler standing southpaw, his hands gloved and ready to strike, a twinkle of hope in his eye.

"Really?" William said, genuinely interested.

"Yeah, in another life. Big shot came in eighty seven against DeAngleo Warren." Eugene raised his brow. When William didn't respond, he continued, "He was a heavy weight prospect at the time. Almost everyone I knew was there that night. Don't think any of em actually thought I had a chance in hell." He laughed. "Turns out they were right. The ref stopped it in the fourth."

Eugene sat in the recliner in the center of the room.

"I buckled him in the second. I was just waiting. If I woulda only connected my left uppercut. Missed him by less than an inch." He looked up at the picture. "Strange how a few seconds can determine a man's destiny."

"I'll have to hear about it in greater details some other time. I'm—"

"Here about Rosemary."

"So you knew her?"

204

"Yeah, she used to come into the gas station. You start shootin' the shit, then you're runnin' into each other everywhere."

"What was the nature of your relationship?"

Eugene scratched his stubble. "We weren't sleepin' together, if that's what you're askin'. I'm old enough to be her father. Maybe even her grandfather."

"Okay, so were you two getting—"

"No, not sayin' I'm no angel. Definitely been down some dead ends." Eugene paused. "I guess I was tryin' to look out for her where I could, you know. She had an enigmatic charisma. People were drawn to her. Not all of em good. And she was battling her own demons."

"Can you verify where you were the night she died?"

"Workin'."

"So when was the last time you saw her?"

Eugene nervously rubbed his hands together.

"Might as well have out with it now. If you really cared for your friend, like you say," William said.

"She knew I was an ex-boxer, and . . ." Eugene glanced at an Ali/Frazier poster to his left. "I've acquired a reputation. Outside the ring. People talk."

"Meaning?"

"Meaning I've made money in the past doing bad things. Mostly to bad people."

"You were a hit man."

Eugene chuckled. "I was the last measure of resolution—a mediator. Rosemary hired me as a bodyguard. She was afraid someone was out to kill her."

"Who? You know who?"

"Leon Hutchins. Owed him some back pay for some cook. But I think he was just obsessed with her."

"They together?"

"Not the way she told it—that wasn't the set up. It wasn't his charm that drew her to him. Leon let that slide as long as they were rolling around, but as soon as she blew him off he started harassing her at work."

"Los Portales?"

Eugene furrowed his brow. "Romeo's."

"She was strippin' there?"

"Yeah, that's where they met. Leon has connections with Romeo."

"You said she hired you?"

"She was scared. Saturday before she died I went out there and waited for her shift to end. Which wasn't unusual, I often went out there after work to make sure nobody was fuckin' with her.

"Leon came in with some people I didn't recognize. Some Mexican with a neck tattoo. Looked dangerous. A business-type woman. Mexican too, I believe. Scar above her lip. She was with some other man, but I couldn't see his face.

"I was gonna do it right there in the field behind the joint, but when I saw Leon there with these people I started having second thoughts and went to find Rosemary.

"I asked a few of the dancers if they'd seen her. One of em told me she went to the back to freshen up. When I rushed to the VIP door, two security guards stopped me. This was odd. Honestly, I don't have much love for Romeo. He's a scumbag, but he never kept me from going to the dressing room area. He seemed to welcome the extra muscle."

"So that was it?"

Eugene smiled slightly. "I barreled through the door anyway. The security guards didn't like that much and we had it out in the hallway. After I tucked them in, I searched Romeo's office. Nobody was there. I trucked it out the back exit just in time to see two cars leaving the parking lot onto the frontage road. One of em Romeo's."

William scrawled in his notepad and then looked at Eugene. "You ever see her again?"

Eugene's eyes welled up with tears. He shook his head.

William descended the rickety stairs, shoving his hands into his jacket, and made his way to his car parked on the street. At the door, Romeo's phone rang from his jacket. He felt it rumble against his hand. He quickly opened the door and hopped inside, pulling the phone out and shutting the door behind him. The chorus from "Cat Scratch Fever" blared from the phone. William looked at the caller.

Robert.

He answered and the music stopped.

"Romeo. We need to meet," said the voice on the other end. Apparently, Robert.

"Really, what about?"

"You know what about—who is this?"

"This is Romeo's cousin, Alfonso. Romeo's dead. We have his shit."

The man on the line swore and hung up.

Robert stopped himself just short of throwing the phone against the barn. Cocksucker. Who could have known about Romeo and the stash? He paced against the barn for a few moments, swearing to himself.

He stormed across the yard when Dennis' truck pulled up the drive. Dennis jumped out with that shit-eating grin on his face. Floyd emerged from the passenger side, a huge bandage on the left side of his neck.

"All better," Dennis said, thumbing to Floyd's direction.

"Everyone in the barn! I'll be there in a minute," Robert called.

He ignored their confused looks and climbed the stairs of the porch. The floorboards creaked under his weight as he reached the side door. He swung it open and charged in.

Carson was still at the kitchen table.

"Thirteen," the boy said as Robert blew by him on the way to the bedroom.

Robert marched upstairs to the dresser and pulled open the top drawer. Grabbed the Arcus 98DA and the case of ammo. He lifted up his flannel and shoved the gun into the back of his pants. Then he returned to the kitchen.

"Thirteen, dad."

"Huh?"

"Thirteen."

"What?!"

"Balloons. That's the answer."

Robert managed a terse smile. "That's right. Self-reliance, son. Don't underestimate its importance."

He patted Carson's shoulder and continued on to the door.

23

The drive-in was halfway between Black River and Hegemony, about a thirty minute drive from Esmeralda's compound. Carlos parked along the grassy shoulder on a dead stretch of asphalt. The frontage road ran parallel to Route 13, mostly reserved for farmers that lived along it or kids killing time on weekends.

He exited and strolled to the back of the black SUV where he popped the hatchback and heaved the black suitcase to the ground. Once on the asphalt, Carlos extended the trolley handle and closed the hatchback. He hit a button on the key ring, locking the vehicle with a beep, and began to walk toward the entrance of the theatre. The suitcase wheels rumbled behind him.

He crossed the pavement onto the gravel entrance, and dragging the suitcase through this terrain turned out to be so shaky that he decided to simply carry it by the strap. So much for the 80mm inline wheels' guarantee of a smooth and stable roll. The suitcase actually cost nearly five hundred, and Carlos had argued the expense should have been subtracted from of the two hundred and fifty thousand, but there was no talking

Queenie into it. Always the best. Beyond that, she told him, it wouldn't matter in the end.

He stopped for a moment. Reached into his jacket for a piece of gum. He stood there calmly, unwrapped it, and stuck it into his mouth. After a few chews he re-folded the aluminum packaging and returned it to his pocket. Then he grabbed the suitcase's strap, lifted it, and continued up the drive.

Carlos approached the arched sign that read Buffalo Superior Drive-In. Written in an old timey font, the blue background and gold trim were sun-bleached. He had to stand fairly close for the words to be legible. As he passed under the arch, he couldn't help but feel like he was entering a cemetery of sorts.

Up ahead, in the midst of oxidized drive-in speakers and cracked concrete where weeds now grew, he saw two men with shotguns. One of them wore a green John Deere hat. The other wore a smile like a simple-minded angel had touched him once when he was a child. A dusty GMC truck rested nearby. Behind them, the giant screen cut a crumbling rectangle in the sky. Stained with yellows and browns and grays, the once white forty-eight foot slab looked like a pair of old underwear.

He gnawed his gum as he trekked through the obliterated vista, maintaining a silence that verged on reverence.

"A'ight, amigo, go ahead and put it down right there," John Deere said when Carlos closed the gap to twenty feet.

Carlos stopped but he didn't set down the suitcase.

"Hey—you hear us, Jose?" The other one said. "Put. The. Suitcase. Down."

Carlos stared at them.

Both men cocked their shotguns.

Carlos nodded, slowly let go of the suitcase, and raised his hands.

"Now take ten steps back," John Deere said.

Carlos followed the instruction, easing backward with his hands in the air, not taking his eyes off the men.

"Wait there just a sec . . ." John Deere nodded to his partner. "Dennis."

The one called Dennis ran forward, somewhat uneasily, and unzipped the suitcase. After checking several bundles of cash, he smiled and nodded to his friend.

"Stay there. Just like that," Dennis said, back by John Deere's side.

"We gonna head out here out the back way and you're gonna walk yo ass back the way you came. If you move before we're outta sight, we will shoot you. Comprende?"

Carlos nodded.

John Deere collected the suitcase, swinging it over his shoulder, and then spun around to the passenger side of the truck. There was a swagger in Dennis' step now, and he kept his gun pointed at Carlos as he strode to the driver's side. He hopped in the truck and they tore off across the empty field beyond the screen.

Carlos could see Dennis look back at him more than once until they were out of sight.

When they had gone, Carlos whirled his finger in the air eastward to Thiago who had been watching the

212

entire exchange five hundred yards away via sniper scope from some brush outside the drive-in.

Carlos entered the black SUV and retrieved a small GPS from the glove compartment. He switched it on and thumbed a button. On the screen, an area map zoomed in to the drive-in. After a few seconds, a red tracking icon bleeped its way along a country road. He set the device on the passenger seat.

He picked up his phone and dialed Esmeralda.

"Tenemos rojo," he said as she answered.

Roland slid into the passenger seat.

"What's up, Willie?" he said.

"The teaching of impermanence, the teaching of non-self, they are instruments for us to practice deep looking. And by looking we discover the nature of inter-being. When we look at a flower—"

Roland smirked, the left side of his cheek dimpling, and said, "This shit again?"

William turned the volume down, and handed Roland a piece of paper.

"Nem—Nembutal?" He paused and then looked at William. "I'll put out some feelers."

"The sooner the better."

"Right, right. I'll let you—get back at you ASAP."

"Also, there's this." William handed him a mug shot of Leon.

Roland eyed the picture for less than a second. "Shit. Leon?"

"Know him?"

"Not exactly."

"Whaddya know?"

"He's *the* guy in Black River. It's real—strictly the shit—top shelf fire, you—you know. Not your usual home—regional kitchen cook. Its gospel—walk on water, turn water to wine tw—tweak. His local crew moves it. Georgie Boy and Frank were his main guys. Doesn't deal directly with anybody else. Snor—had it but, never fucked much with em in person. There could be—might be others—a few smaller guys on the food ch—the pecking order."

"Really?" William chewed on his nail. "Big Deal one of em?"

"Big Douche?!" Roland laughed, and then thought it over. "Could be." He shrugged.

"He turned up dead. Brains plastered on his kitchen wall."

"And the Grass brothers—Leon's a dangerous dude."

"Heard a rumor," William said, and then hesitated. "Rosemary was shackin' up with him."

Roland shook his head as if to clear a bad image. "Heard the sam—People talked shortly after she split."

"You know who he's affiliated with?"

"Dunno. Somebody—some connect up in Hegemony."

William pulled the car from the curb, Roland's mother's house disappearing in the rearview.

"Where we goin'?"

Before they'd reached the end of his mother's block, Roland switched out the dharma talk with the Stooges' *Fun House* and cranked the volume. Both men grinned.

From the highway, William watched the orange sun bleed away into night.

"1970" had hit its avant-punk crescendo—Steve Mackay's sax going ape shit—by the time they arrived at the Wolfe farm. William let it play out, the headlights making monstrous shadows of smooth brome and witchgrass. With his arm out the window, Roland hammered out the beat against the door.

William stamped out his cigarette in the ashtray and opened his door. "Come on, let's go."

"We're not going insi—in the house, are we? I mean—I love your parents—I just can't do it, man."

"No." William popped the trunk and then stepped from the car, leaving the lights on.

"Where are we goin' then?"

"Just come on."

William stalked to the trunk, fished out two Maglites, and handed one to Roland. Then he led them into the tall grass, slowing his stride to ensure his friend's feet wouldn't tangle up in the weeds. He stopped at the barn door. With the flashlight steadied in his armpit, he turned the gold-plated padlock upright and dialed in the four-digit combination.

Inside, they maneuvered around a pair of bikes, a riding lawnmower, duct-taped boxes, antiques, bric-a-brac, tools, and half-refinished furniture. Organized in

215

long rows down the center of the barn, and collected against the left wall, salvaged wood awaited Lionel's next project.

A refrigerator stood at the back wall. William headed to it.

"This thing hasn't worked since before we were born," he said. He pointed to his father's workbench. "Turn that light on over there, would you?"

Roland ambled over to the workbench and switched on the table lamp. William swung open the refrigerator, hoisting a duffle bag up onto the workbench. He unzipped the bag and flipped over the flap.

Roland stared at him in awe.

William lifted a Ziploc from the duffle bag, placed it on the workbench. With a knife from his jacket, he cut away part of the plastic and collected a small amount on the blade. He snorted it, repeated the process and carefully handed the blade to a wide-eyed Roland.

Roland eagerly took the knife and imbibed the powder.

He sighed. "That's the shit. That's it." He eyed William for a moment. "Damn, Willie. This is—this is a death sentence, you know?"

"Want out?"

"Fuck no."

24

From the couch behind the coffee table, Tidy Cat slouched forward with her eyebrows raised and waited for Roland to make a decision.

He eyed the array of handguns laid out in front of him. They more or less looked the same. He glanced at Charlie Biscuits, who shrugged from the doorway before taking a bite of his candy bar.

Roland picked one from the middle, gripped it in his hand, ran Polanski over the trigger. There were slight nicks in the metal, some wear on the grip. It felt comfortable enough. "This one," he said, gazing up at Tidy Cat.

She grinned and scratched her shaved head. "Good choice. Sig Sauger P220. Never fails to feed and fire. Absolute stopping power. Mag holds eight rounds and one in the chamber. Only choice for hardcore special forces units."

Only thing Roland knew about Tidy Cat was how she got her nickname. According to Biscuits, she'd once spent four hours scouring the carpet for crank crumbs on her hands and knees. Ended up smoking kitty litter.

She had three dots tattooed over her left brow, like ellipsis or markings from some strange cult. He could make out her nipples through a gray wifebeater. Also, she didn't shave her pits.

"What do you—how much?"

Tidy Cat clicked her tongue. "Since you're a friend of Biscuits, I'll give it to you for seven."

"Ammo?"

"Two for one."

Roland's eyes shifted from Tidy Cat to Biscuits. "I'm looking to—need to—unload some shit. Either of you interested?"

Tidy Cat sighed. "Depends on what we're talkin'."

Roland bent down to the messenger bag at his boots. He unloaded a bindle from the side pocket, cut two lines on the table.

After snorting his sample, and while Tidy Cat took her turn, Biscuits beat his chest Tarzan-style and roared. "God damn," he said, rolling his head from shoulder to shoulder. "God. Damn."

Roland waited.

"There's no way you cooked this," Tidy Cat said when she was done.

"I didn't—never said I did. Just need to move it ASAP."

Biscuits eyed Roland suspiciously. "What you up to, Roland? Buying guns—never seen you strapped, even back in the day. Now you sellin' primo shit. What's up?"

"Leon Hutchins's goin'—takin' a hit. A big one. And you can quote me. Let people—Get the word out."

"Shit. You're one crazy motherfucker," Tidy Cat said.

Biscuits' eyes popped open, a big stupid grin broke out over his face. "Roland's finally growin' a pair."

Tidy Cat slipped a cigarette into the corner of her mouth and raised an eyebrow. "Maybe, but he's gonna need more guns. How bout a trade?"

William sat on the living room couch, drinking a bottle of Templeton Rye. After a long swig, he set the whiskey on the floor and picked up his phone from the coffee table. He opened his contacts. Angie's number was first. He stared at it for a moment and then tapped the screen. He stood up, inhaled heavily, and put the phone to his ear. It rang. He almost ended the call then.

It rang again.

"Hello," she answered.

"Hey, Angie." His voice came out weak.

"Oh. Hello."

"I was wonderin' if I could speak to him."

Silence, and then, "Oh, shoot, he's sleeping right now."

"It's five—he's sleeping already?"

"Yeah, he's taking a nap. He *is* only seven."

"Right. Well, did he get the package I—"

"Okay, I'll tell him you called. I'm sure he'll be *really* sad he missed it, since he never hears from you," she said.

"That's total bullsh—"

The line went dead.

William tossed the phone to the couch. Kicked the coffee table. It slid across the hardwood floor and smashed into the wall.

Bottles and cigarette ash toppled to the floor.

As they hit a bump, Leon's head bobbed and smacked the truck bed. He swore, adjusting his shoulders, hands still bound, and tried to hold up his neck. They hit another bump and his head bounced off cool metal again. Fuckwit One and Fuckwit Two chuckled from the cab.

He rolled onto his side, wiggling vigorously in an attempt to ditch the burlap. When that didn't work, he pushed himself up onto his knees. The truck rocked, causing him to lose balance and almost collapse back to the floor, but he managed to stay upright by spreading his legs farther apart. Then he swung himself back and forth, a motion he had to admit probably looked like he was violently going to town on an eighteen inch cock.

Whatever. It did the trick.

The burlap sack flew from his head—last glimpse as it flapped in the taillights before disappearing out into the night. The truck rocketed along some back road. Nothing but wind and stars. The latter touched something in Leon that he could neither articulate nor had the desire to.

"Hey, now," Fuckwit Two hollered out the open passenger window. "Sit back." He said something to the other, and the truck swerved right onto the grassy shoulder and stopped.

The two men hurdled out the vehicle.

"Might as well leave 'im here then," Fuckwit One said, wrenching down the tailgate while the other leapt inside the truck bed to get at Leon. He kicked wildly as they hauled him out the back and dropped him in the grass. One of them drove a knee between his shoulders, holding him in place. The other cut the zip tie.

220

Leon immediately shot up from the ground and lurched for them. Both men danced out of range.

Fuckwit One pulled a revolver. "Let's be smart."

Leon paused, arms stretched skyward, and the men retreated to the truck.

Doors slammed in unison. The truck zoomed down the road, spraying dust in its wake.

Fifty feet ahead, its break lights suddenly flashed and it reversed, going into the shoulder, and then turned around headed in Leon's direction. He stared into the headlights and half-expected them to run him over, but they blew past with a honk of the horn.

Leon flipped them the bird.

He had been walking for close to an hour when another car approached. Its beams came slow over the dark road and he knew then who it was. A few minutes later, the black SUV stopped in front of him. Leon stood in the bright light, hand cupped over his eyes to see.

Carlos got out of the car with his gun drawn.

He could have run then—hell, he could have run when the car was a mile away—but he didn't. He simply raised his arms in a defeated sort of way and stepped to the passenger door. He sat down, his body sinking into the seat, and leaned his head back on the headrest.

Without looking at Carlos, he said, "All right, then."

Carlos closed his door and continued down the road. They traveled the length of the road Leon had walked. He stared out the passenger window and watched the dark field move by. They passed a gravel driveway that lead up to small house. The porch light was on.

They reached a stop sign after several more miles. Leon wiped at the dried blood on his lip with his sleeve and said, "Need some cigarettes. They took everything. My phone and wallet."

Carlos said nothing. He turned right onto the crossroad. Leon wondered how many miles they had traveled like this over the course of their association. Stoic motherfucker, Carlos was.

Another fifteen minutes rolled by and they entered a town called What Cheer. Leon recognized the name—it was the exit before Hegemony—and he always wondered what made the town so happy. The only reasons to name a place What Cheer would be if tweak blew in the wind like pollen and pussy packed every corner. Looking at it now as they drove through, it was no different than every other dogshit town in Iowa.

Carlos pulled into a Casey's and parked. From his black suit coat, he took out his wallet and handed Leon a twenty.

Leon nodded in thanks, got out of the car, and walked into the gas station.

"Pisser?" he asked the clerk.

The woman behind the counter glanced up from a crossword, nodded to the right. Leon strode to the bathroom and took a long piss. Then he stood at the mirror and checked his look. He still had dried blood in the corner of his mouth. A pink welt was forming under his left eye. There were several cuts. One on his cheek. Another near the crown of his head. Dirt stained his suit here and there, but he didn't look *that* bad. He splashed hot water over his face a few times, making sure to clean off the blood, and ran his wet hands through his hair.

When he was done he stopped at the front counter.

"Marlboro Reds."

The woman retrieved the cigarettes from behind her.

"Oh, and a lighter," he said, slapping the pack against his palm. She handed him a Bic. While she was ringing him up, he opened the pack, discarded the cellophane on the counter, and lit a cigarette.

Her eyes widened. "Sir, you can't smoke in here."

Back in the SUV, Leon cracked the window, exhaling a shotgun blast of smoke, and gave Carlos his change. "Much better. Thanks."

Carlos returned to the main road.

They crossed a set of train tracks, heading east out of town. Leon saw the sign for Route 13 when they hit a red light. He scanned the area. A closed corner café. Arvin Plumbing and Heating across the street. No cars. No people.

He exhaled another flurry of smoke.

Then he swung across the seat and stamped out his cigarette on Carlos' cheek. Carlos grunted, reeled in his seat, and instinctively brought his hands up to cover his face. At the same time, Leon grabbed his bald head and pounded it against the driver side window. In a daze, and trying to escape, Carlos pushed open the car door. The two men toppled to the pavement, Leon landing on top.

He again grabbed Carlos' head and beat it into the street. Carlos flailed, uselessly attempting to stop the onslaught with weak blows to Leon's arms. Leon seized the gun from inside Carlos' coat and shot him once between the eyes, quickly rummaged his old associate's pockets, located his wallet, then jumped into the black SUV, and floored it to Route 13 headed south to Black River.

25

It was close to ten by the time the Crimley household sat down to eat dinner. Being something of a celebration, Robert had invited Dennis and Howard, and their respective partners, Liz and Stephanie. Tonya had spent the day in the kitchen and a small feast filled the table: three plates of her revered fried chicken, a big bowl of mashed potatoes and a side of gravy, apple slaw, green bean casserole, and hot dinner rolls with melted butter and honey. After Robert led the guests in prayer, everyone passed around the dishes and ate in silence. Even Carson, usually talkative among company, remained quiet, concentrating on his drumsticks.

Once dinner finished, Robert helped the women clear the table and wash the dishes. Floyd finally came into the house (he'd been stewing in the garage since his return from the hospital) and both Robert and Tonya offered him food, but he only grumbled and stormed away.

A half-hour later Robert walked into the living room, and found Dennis and Howard sitting on the couch, taking long pulls from cheap beers. Floyd iced his bandaged neck from a ragged recliner with a bad air about him. He slouched way down in the seat, and stared grimly at the TV.

"Leon got you good—didn't he, Floyd?" Dennis said.

Floyd didn't take his eyes from the screen. "How 'bout you shut the fuck up and make yourself useful."

"Huh?" Dennis leaned forward evidently not hearing or not understanding.

Floyd rocketed an empty beer can across the room. It bounced off Dennis' forehead and tinged into a corner. Dennis recoiled and yelped, rubbing his brow. Howard snickered and adjusted his faded John Deere hat. A smile cracked the corner of Floyd's mouth.

"Well?" Floyd said after Dennis didn't get up.

"Well, what?"

"Get up and get me goddamn beer."

"I ain't gettin' you a beer. You can get it yourself."

Floyd glared at Dennis. "Get up and get me a beer."

"I'll get it," Robert said and went to the refrigerator.

He came back and tossed the cold one to Floyd, who caught it and nodded in approval. He popped the tab and took a swig. Robert cut through the living room and climbed the stairs to the second floor. He stopped at Carson's room and leaned his head in.

Carson sat on his floor playing with Hot Wheels.

"You ought to brush your teeth and hit the hay," Robert said.

He continued down the hall to the bedroom, opened the closet door, and fetched the black suitcase, laying it on the bed. After unzipping the small carry-on,

Robert gazed down at the money for a moment and smiled. Two hundred and fifty thousand. He went about counting the money again for a third time, running a thumbnail along each edge of currency strap before dropping it on the comforter. Each strap contained a hundred one hundred dollar bills. He had gotten through the first hundred thousand when heard one of the women scream downstairs.

Tossing the money onto the bed, Robert lumbered to the door and leaned his head out into the hallway. He could make out yelling, but didn't recognize the voice. It sounded like Spanish.

He stepped out of the bedroom, hoping to discern who was speaking. As he did, gunfire erupted through the house.

He pulled the piece from the back of his waistband and ran down the hall, shouting at Carson to stay in his room, and hopping down the steps four at a time. At the bottom of the stairs, he scrambled into the living room. Three men in black paramilitary garb had assault rifles pointed at Howard, Dennis, and Floyd. Robert fired at the one closest to him, hitting the man in neck. The man buckled and fell into the wall. One of the other men returned fire and a bullet ripped through Robert's thigh. He dropped to the floor, his gun falling from his hand. At the same time, Floyd lurched from the recliner to grab a handgun on the coffee table. The third man let off a spurt from his rifle that sent Floyd back into the seat with a chest full of lead. Howard and Dennis froze on the couch. Robert lunged for his weapon. The man that shot him raced forward and kicked the gun away. He raised his hands. Three more men entered the room.

There were eight in all and they drug Robert and his men and women from the house out into the yard. The women cried and pleaded as the men arranged them all in a line on their knees. Two black SUVs drove up the thin drive, white headlights pouring over their faces. The second car pulled off into the grass and parked. Robert squinted and saw a figure emerge from the backseat. The silhouette advanced across the yard and into the porch light, and he saw that it was Esmeralda Castillo. At her side, she carried a machete.

From the side of the house, one of her men gathered the stump Robert used to cut wood and brought it back and positioned it near him at the end of the line. Then she motioned to her men and they pulled Dennis from the line and forced his head onto the stump.

"Go fuck yerself, bitch," he said.

Esmeralda held her gaze on Robert, her eyes filled with some wild terror. With both hands, she raised the machete above her head and brought it down in one swift motion against Dennis' neck. His head fell from the stump into the grass. The women cried out.

"I wanted to be here, looking into your eyes, while you watch your people die," Esmeralda said.

Behind her, the screen door slammed. Tonya screamed. Another of Esmeralda's men was pulling Carson down the steps. The boy tried to jerk free. He kicked at the man's shins and wildly swung his body about.

The man backhanded him across the face.

Carson cried out.

Tonya jumped from the line and ran toward him. Esmeralda's men shot her in the back, and then, without pause, turned and killed the other women.

"No . . . Please . . . I'm sorry . . . What can I do?" Robert pleaded.

The man with Carson reached Esmeralda's side. The boy's nose was bloody. Tears streamed down his cheeks.

The corner of Esmeralda's top lip twitched. "We're beyond negotiating," she said, tightening her grip on the machete.

They were somewhere outside Hegemony. The road was long and the landscape amorphous, the blackness seemed to continually transform into darker fields and hills around them. Robert sat in the middle of the backseat, between two indistinguishable soldiers, with his hands tied behind him. Another two sat in the front. It was quiet except for the sound of the engine and the clang of gravel ricocheting off the wheel wells. He watched the road through the windshield, half-hypnotized as they accelerated over rocks and dirt, and he wondered more than once if he was dreaming.

Finally, they turned on to what Robert thought was a driveway. It took him several minutes to realize they were moving across an open field toward a house. As they closed the gap, his mind returned to what he'd witnessed. Not more than two hours before, he had been sitting with them at the kitchen table. Now everyone he loved was dead, slaughtered like animals in his front yard. On his own land. But he felt nothing. Instead, a great numbness had engulfed him. The world had moved beyond his grasp. The SUV bobbed over unlevel earth and the men bounced in their seats.

When they arrived at the house, the two men in the backseat yanked him out into the night. He turned, nervously looking for the other two men, and saw they had gathered at the back of the vehicle. One of them lifted something—it looked to Robert like a giant box— from the hatchback. Then he couldn't see.

They led him, limping from the shot to his leg, into the remnants of a long abandoned farmhouse half-destroyed by fire.

Smoke damage blackened the walls. Dust covered charred furniture.

"Where are you taking me?" Robert asked, not expecting an answer, but feeling the need to speak. "Just shot me and get it over with."

They muscled him down a darkened hallway that led to an empty room. Once inside, one of the men held him down as the other ripped off his clothes. He tried to fight them, but they hit him with the butt of their rifles. Then they duct-taped his ankles together and drug him over to an old radiator and tied him to one of its legs.

"Fuckin' do it, then. Come on. What are you waiting for?" Robert yelled.

The second set of Esmeralda's soldiers entered the room. The first carried a digital video camera and went about setting it upon a tripod. He angled it toward Robert at the radiator. The other man hoisted in the box concealed by a blanket. He set it on the floor. It clanged as if made of metal. Behind the red light of the camera, the man nodded to the others.

All of them withdrew from the room except the man at the box. He pulled back the blanket to reveal a cage full of rats. The man opened the gate and left the room, closing the door behind him, and Robert screamed as dozens of rats vied to exit the cage.

26

A day and a half had passed since Leon left Carlos dead in the streets of What Cheer. A story ran in the newspaper the morning after. Some geriatric walking her dog before sunrise found the body. According to the article, the police had no leads—and indeed, no identity on the victim—and implored the public to come forward with any information.

Tiredness and soul-pulverizing depression were coming on. He needed to get the fuck outta dodge before Esmeralda closed in, but first things first. He'd hit the streets, south Black River, looking to score some Nazi cold. Quality would be an issue, but the town was dry. Besides, beggars couldn't be choosers. He just needed something to tide him over.

But before he got ahead of himself, he needed some scratch.

Wendy, a dancer from X's and O's, lived in an apartment on the south side. Leon pulled up to the complex, parked in a handicapped spot, left the SUV running, and rolled up to the third floor.

He banged on the door endlessly until she answered.

"What the fuck?" she said after she opened the door. She stood in the doorway swathed in a white sheet, her bare shoulders visible. From the looks of it, she hadn't washed her face from the night before. Looked like bat shit was pouring out her eyes.

"Late night, Wendy?" Leon said, pushing his way into the apartment.

"Leon, what are you doing? You just can't—"

"Don't have time to talk. I need some cash."

"I don't have anything."

Leon slapped her across the face. The force of the blow drove her into the wall. The sheet fell from her body. Wendy recoiled and covered her breasts.

"I've seen what you bring in. Now where is it?" Leon yelled.

Wendy wiped at her bleeding lip. "I told you—"

Leon pulled his gun and put it to her head.

"Behind the stereo."

"Good girl." Leon stormed across the room and culled a Ziplock bag from behind an old Yamaha receiver.

"What the fuck is this?"

Leon looked up.

One of the bouncers from Romeo's—he couldn't remember his name—entered the room from the hall, fastening his jeans. After taking stock of Wendy on the ground, the bouncer sailed from the hallway to Leon and threw a haymaker. Leon ducked, and he jacked the bouncer in the nose with the butt of his gun. The bouncer fell to the floor and Leon shot him in the foot.

"Try to get up and the next one's between your eyes." Leon swung back toward Wendy. "I apologize. I didn't know you were entertaining. Now I'll be outta your way, I just need some shit."

"In my purse," Wendy cried, pointing to the table.

Back in the car, Leon snorted what little amount Wendy had. He'd need more. He left the complex and scoured the side streets for anyone who might have something. He stopped a worn down hooker and then a bum, pulling up the SUV next to the sidewalk and hollering at them from the window. Neither had a clue on a connect. Or they didn't trust him.

At day's end, and yielding nothing, Leon rented a room out on Route 13 and spent the night sitting at a small table smoking and gazing out the window down into the parking lot. He didn't sleep a wink and he watched the sun come up.

In the morning, he drove to Denny's and forced himself to eat some toast with his five cups of coffee.

After breakfast, he drove around aimlessly for a few hours. Again, he tried to hit up strangers for some tweak. No luck. Then he remembered Dino, one of his ears on the ground. He leveled the pedal and hustled across town.

Being a man of the people, Dino was out front at his place, talking to a circle of other lowlifes. Leon pulled up and honked. Dino ceased his conversation, waved, and strutted up to the window of the SUV. He wore pale cosmetic foundation that couldn't hide deep acne scars and blue eye shadow that went to dark points at the edges of his eyes. His lips were painted hot rod red. He cropped his hair short like he cut it himself without a mirror and he wore an unwashed white t-shirt, cigarettes rolled up in the left sleeve.

He smiled and leaned his head inside the car. "Hey, sugar. How's Leon doing?"

"Get in."

Dino got in the car.

"I need some shit."

"Leon needs some shit? Why in the world—"

"Don't worry about it. You got something or not?"

"You're in luck. Just scored some last night."

Leon grumbled.

Dino reached into his jeans and handed Leon a bindle. "And it's unbelievable, honey."

Leon snatched the bindle and dumped the entire contents into his cupped hand. Snorted it. Licked his palm.

It took a second to hit him. "Fuck. This is my shit. This is my fucking shit." He pounded the steering wheel.

Dino batted his lashes in confusion.

"Where'd you get this?!" Leon demanded.

"I dunno. Got it through my friend, Gene." He thumbed toward the small crowd and then yelled, "Hey, Gene, come 'ere for a second."

Gene, a kid in his twenties, stomped over to the car. "What?" he said.

Dino lowered his voice a bit. "Where'd you get that?"

Gene eyed Leon. "Don't know what you're talkin' about."

Leon howled.

Dino put a hand on Gene's wrist. "Oh, come on, honey. You know who this is?"

"Nah. I don't give a fuck."

Leon pointed his piece at Gene. "Hey, Gene," he said. "Don't be rude."

"Biscuits."

"Who?"

"Charlie Biscuits."

Charlie Biscuits. Charlie Biscuits. "Who's Charlie Biscuits?"

"Nobody. Just a guy. Lives over on Walter."

Just a guy. Leon turned to Dino, "You know what? Get the fuck out." And then to Gene, "You—you get in."

"Which one is it?" Leon asked as he turned onto Walter Street.

Gene pointed to the duplex a block up. "The white one. Left side."

Leon parked behind a pale blue Caprice. "Time to get gone."

"I've gotta walk back?" Gene protested.

"You think now's a time to be whining about a ride?"

Gene got out of the car, slamming the door, and swiftly walked in the direction they'd come. Leon waited until the kid was half a block away and then he exited the car and hoofed it to the white duplex. He jumped the steps onto the porch and pounded on the door.

"Police—open up," he hollered.

The door opened a few inches. An eye stared out above a chain lock.

Leon shoved his gun into the crack, right in front of the eye, and said, "Charlie Biscuits—open the goddamn door."

The door closed for second and then reopened all the way, revealing a long-haired man with a beard. He stood in a hallway with his shirt off. Leon stomped forward and jabbed the gun into his throat. Then he strong-armed Charlie Biscuits down the hall and threw him on the couch in the living room.

Leon hovered over him. "Who are you and why are you seling my shit?"

"I'm nobody, man."

"That's what they're sayin'. So why you have my product?"

"I don't—I mean I did. A little of it, but I don't have it. I swear."

"Where you get it?"

"Roland, man. He has it all."

Leon eased up some, his face contorting in shock. "Roland? Are you fuckin' kidding me?"

"No, he's got two duffle bags full."

"Roland," Leon said again. "That burnt turd. Where'd he get it?"

"Dunno. He just showed up with it a few days ago. Said it was yours. He's gotta target out for you, or somethin'."

Leon cackled, slapping his thigh. "This just gets better and better. Where can I find him?"

"I don't know where he is now, but I know where he'll be."

A Def Leppard tune caromed inside the Rock Bottom. The place was busy, but not packed. To Roland's surprise, the peanut shells had been swept from the floor. The tile wasn't much to behold. He took his usual place at the end of the bar near the exit and wiped his sweaty palms on his jeans.

Delilah came by and set down a cold Hamm's and a shot of Jameson. He knocked back the shot and sipped at the beer, fidgeting on his stool while he stared at the TVs. Reality shows. Sports. News. On one screen, Lou Ferrigno raged silently—growls buried by choruses of "Pour Some Sugar On Me"—in green-skinned glory and torn shirt. He needed some more courage. He flagged down Delilah with a gnarled hand. She scurried over and refilled his shot glass. He asked her about the peanuts.

"Ray and I saved up some money," she said. "We're gonna re-tile the floor."

"Gettin' fancy on me." He downed the shot.

She went into a story. He tried to follow it, but his mind strayed back to Leon and the gun in his hoodie. Biscuits had phoned immediately after Leon's visit. Apparently, the only reason Biscuits survived was so he could let Roland know Leon planned to skin him alive. After he hung up the phone, Roland had called William, telling him Leon had surfaced and would more than likely make his move at the Rock Bottom.

Delilah smiled and abruptly walked away.

Roland spent the next hour craning his neck toward the door every time a customer entered or exited. He still couldn't feel the booze. His stomach rumbled and turned like a cement mixer. He hadn't shat in six days, but his bowels suddenly felt like they were gonna give way. He hustled to the bathroom, shut the stall door. Ripping strips of toilet paper and laying them on the seat, Roland sat down but nothing came. After a few minutes of waiting, he laid out a bump on the lid of the toilet paper dispenser. He pulled up his pants, leaned down for a quick snort, and then returned to his barstool.

"Roland, you ole bag of flesh."

He turned to the voice as Leon slapped him on the back. Hard.

"Go—go fuck yourself."

Leon frowned. "You still bent outta shape about that whole deal?"

Roland twitched, looking up at a TV screen.

"Come on, that's water under the bridge." Leon thumped the bar top with his fist. "Lemme buy you a drink."

"No, thanks."

Leon shed the fake smile, brown leather creaking as he bent to Roland's good ear. He whispered, "Know what, Vern? She was beggin' for it when she came to my door. Said she needed a real fuck after having to put up with your limp, over-cooked, cocktail weenie for so long." Leon shook his pinkie in the air. "Oh," he said, rocking away from Roland's ear and raising his voice, "you owe me five hundred on that abortion."

The color went out of Roland's face. He peered into Leon's eyes, looking for any indication of lies. He didn't find any.

"You didn't know?" Leon said in feigned sympathy. "She couldn't wait to rip that thing out of her."

Roland leapt from the barstool and shoved Leon, who tottered backward and fell to the floor. Then Roland exploded toward him, dropping to his knees and connecting with a fist to the face. Leon threw a punch to defend himself, but it missed, and Roland swung his fists down upon him.

Leon absorbed most of the shots with his forearm and thrust an open palm into Roland's chin, forcing him back into a barstool. Leon pulled Roland up with him as he got to his feet, grabbing his skinny arms and pushing him into the bar.

Roland registered Delilah's frantic motion behind the bar in his peripheral and heard her yell to Ray. He tried to free himself from Leon's grip and thrust his weight to the side. The two toppled into the exit door and onto the pavement outside. Leon dragged him across the pavement, punishing him with blows to the head.

Ray stormed through the exit into the alley. He lurched toward Leon, but Leon jerked away and pulled his gun.

"Stop—you're gonna kill him," Ray shouted.

Leon panted. "That's the fuckin' idea."

"Not here it ain't. I don't care what you do, but not here."

Roland writhed on the ground, struggling unsuccessfully to get to his feet. He reached into his hoodie.

240

Blood dripped from Leon's nose. "We're gonna go for a ride and you're gonna wish you burnt up in that fire."

Before Roland could draw the gun, Leon punted him across the temple with a boot heel. Roland's head snapped back and his vision swirled away into darkness.

He came to in the backseat of an SUV. Black leather seats. New car smell. Up front, Leon white knuckled the wheel, cigarette smoke whipping out the open window. Next to him, in the passenger seat, Rosemary flipped a strand of hair behind her ear. She laughed at something Leon said. Looked upon him like he was the king of the world.

Roland could feel the warmth of tears, and then the world went black again.

27

Leon traveled east on Foster, crossing Black River bridge, and continued on to the long entrance of the Iowa Meat Packaging plant. On the dark road, the black SUV rolled over pavement punctured by harsh weeds and purred up to the deserted facility. Its brick exterior, tagged by years of aspiring graffiti artists, stood in ruin. Where windows weren't completely shattered, the glass was veiled in a thick layer of dust.

Leon stretched between the front seats and smacked Roland. "Get out." Then he grabbed his bag of tricks from the passenger seat, and clambered out of the car. Leon clicked on a Maglite he'd found in the glove box and tugged Roland, wrists zip-tied, from the back.

It was colder inside—a damp hopeless kind of cold. The place smelled of mildew and rot, an undercurrent of death still clinging to the walls. They marched through the black rooms, Leon's flashlight revealing filthy industrial processing machines, broken assembly lines, meat hooks, prep stations, cobwebbed hallways, puddles of dirty water, warped and destroyed drywall, rolls of weather-stained insulation that had dropped from the ceiling.

They came to an open area where brick and mortar had divided and crumbled. The ceiling and the far wall had collapsed, brick blackened by fire, and the room opened to night. Patina formed on wrenched metal. Steel pillars, rusted to shades of brown red, rose from moss-covered rubble, and ropes dangled from skeletal rafters.

Leon pushed Roland forward. "Keep goin'."

They moved into the giant room, Leon pulling at the back of Roland's hoodie, occasionally prodding him on with the end of the Maglite. At a hobo camp near the room's center, Leon forced Roland into a folding beach chair. He dropped his bag next to a fire pit lined in stones and combed the room for wood, keeping his eye on Roland as he moved. He carried back several armfuls of scrap wood and dumped them in the pit. When he was done, Leon crouched down and dug out lighter fluid from the bag and squirted the liquid on the wood and ignited the fire with the lighter he bought in What Cheer. The fire burned low and blue, the wood sizzled and bubbled at the ends.

"Too wet," Roland mumbled.

"It'll burn," Leon said, dousing the pile in another shot of lighter fluid. The fire flared for a moment. "Just like you."

Leon seized a metal shard from his feet and set one end in the fire. He held his hands over the pit and stared into the flames for some time.

"It don't matter much one way or other, but I didn't kill her," he said finally, not taking his eyes off the fire.

"I don't believe you." Roland twitched in the seat. Leon couldn't tell if ol' crater face was on the verge of tears or what. Maybe it was just a spasm.

"Well, like I said, it don't matter one way or other." Leon raised the metal shard from the fire. The tip glowed orange. He looked at Roland. "I need to know where my drugs are, Roland. The sooner I do, the sooner you can join her." He stood up and approached Roland, holding the metal shard. "Otherwise, it's gonna be a long night."

As Leon took a step toward Roland, William emerged from the shadows, gun drawn. "Drop it."

"Ah, the farm boy then. Heard so much," Leon said, managing a smile.

William fired a warning shot to some debris at Leon's feet, causing him to flinch and drop the metal shard.

"All right. Easy." Leon slowly raised his arms.

William side-stepped a pile of bricks and strode forward. "Get on your—"

Before William could get out the words, Leon dove into his coat pocket, retrieving his piece, and returned fire in one swift motion. William ducked and the shot missed, the sound echoing in the facility. Leon scurried over the rubble and out the crumbled wall into the night.

William leapt to Roland, cutting him loose. "Get out of here. Go."

Then William took after Leon through the wall.

Outside, he managed the rock and debris that had collected on a small hill leading to train tracks below. Halfway down the hill, he stumbled on loose rubble and began to slide.

Roland limped away from the hobo camp into the dark interior of IMP. Without a flashlight, areas of the facility were pitch black. He came to the room with assembly line hooks. The moon shown through a giant spread of window panes. He rounded a corner and raked his shin on a pile of rock and metal and fell to the floor with a grunt. He cursed in frustration and examined his hand. A few droplets of blood in his palm. He reached out with his other hand for balance, trying to boost up from the floor, and felt a cold pipe. It was the length of a Louisville Slugger, thin enough for his stubs to grasp around it.

Leon ran between the train ties, his boots sinking in the ballast. He glanced back. The detective had slid to the bottom of the hill and was getting up. Leon abruptly stopped and fired. Dinged to the left of the detective.

The detective answered the shot. It whizzed past Leon into the gravel ahead.

Leon broke out into a run again. He could hear shots ping around him. After a few yards, he hopped off the train tracks to the right into a ditch that went back up into the hill. Clutching clumps of muddy grass in his fists, he clawed his way up. Rock fell beneath his feet and mud stained his suit pants as he crawled over the top of the ledge.

He ran through tall grass to the entrance road and, breathing heavily, double-backed toward the meat packing plant. He could hear nothing but his panting and his boot heels clomping on the black top. In the midst of his stride, he reeled around several times to see if the detective was behind him. Nothing.

As he closed in on the plant, he could see the detective's car parked behind the black SUV. He hustled to the door, groping for his keys.

"Goin' somewhere, Vern?"

Leon wheeled around in time to see a swinging pipe connect with his chest. The air went out of his lungs and he dropped to the pavement. Then Roland was over him, striking him in the face with his gimp paws. The detective came out of the dark and bear-hugged Roland from behind and heaved him to the side before spinning Leon onto his chest and slapping a pair of cuffs on his wrists.

Leon spit a glob of blood into the night and closed his eyes.

William stood next to a squad car, thumbed to Leon Hutchins in the backseat. "Go ahead and take him on in to the interview room. I'll be there shortly."

"Where you goin'?" Darwin Cash asked.

"I'm gonna take Roland home."

Darwin nodded and walked around the car. William saluted Leon, who stared at him blankly. He walked by another squad car, waved at Widy behind the

246

wheel. Roland was sitting on the walkway that lead up to the IMP plant, smoking, and surveying the town beyond the train tracks. He looked pensive and exhausted.

"You ready, killer?" he asked.

Roland nodded.

They traveled back along the entrance road, turned left on Foster heading toward town. The moon illuminated the fields next to the highway. They didn't speak.

When they came to Black River Bridge, Roland said, "Can just let me out here." His voice was almost inaudible.

"Sure?"

"Yeah, man. I just wanna walk for awhile. Clear my head."

William stopped in front of the bridge and put the car in park. "You gonna be okay?"

Roland stared at the bridge. "You know—she was going to—she was pregnant. I was gonna be a father. But she decided to . . . ." He turned to William with tears in his eyes. "Maybe it would have made a difference."

"Maybe." William didn't know what else to say, so he didn't. After a moment, he said, "Why don't I take you to my place? You can crash there."

Roland shook his head. "I'm all right. I'll be fine. I wanna watch the river for a bit." He opened the door and got out of the car. And then changing tone, "Oh, I almost forgot—" He fished around in his hoodie pocket and handed William a bottle of pills.

"What's this?"

"Got it on trade."

William glanced at the bottle and then put it on the passenger seat. "Thank you."

"We should go fishing sometime . . . if you're up for it."

"We should. How 'bout tomorrow?"

"Til then." Roland closed the door.

William pulled away. He looked up into the rearview. Roland was still standing in the road, watching the car pass over the bridge.

28

William entered the interview room with a cup of water and two aspirin. He set the cup down on the table and dropped the pills in Leon's palm.

"For your headache," he said, taking a seat.

"How'd you know?"

William shrugged. "Could see it in your face."

Leon popped the pills in his mouth, sipped the water.

"So where we at here, Leon?"

"Whaddya mean?"

"Rosemary Montgomery."

"I didn't kill her is where we're at."

"Maybe, maybe not. But word is you were with Rosemary the last time anybody saw her."

"Whose word?"

"Eugene Standler places you with Rosemary at X's and O's."

"That old love sick puppy? Please. Besides, it's circumstantial at best. Good luck with that."

"What I got is kidnapping and attempted murder on a police officer. You're lookin' at some serious time."

Leon sighed, cracked his knuckles. "How bout I tell you what I know and you let me walk outta here."

William laughed. "You're a funny guy."

Leon scratched at his chin and then leaned back in his chair. He was silent. William could see the air go out of him in that moment. Leon looked almost pensive.

"Well?"

"What the hell? I need a cigarette . . . then I'll tell you what happened. We're dead men anyway."

William delved into his jacket for his cigarettes. He handed one to Leon and lit one for himself. "As long as we're breaking the rules."

Leon grabbed the lighter and lit his own. He took a drag, savoring the smoke as it entered his lungs, and exhaled slowly and completely. "California sent us a chemist on loan. Esmeralda was to set up a super lab."

"Esmeralda your supplier?"

"Esmeralda Castillo is *the* supplier in the region. She'd charmed California and they were in awe of her, yadda yadda. She wasn't just gonna to be a regional distributor. She'd cornered the market. California was only okay with this because Queenie would still be importing a percentage from them. It was a diplomatic move. She would have her cake and eat it too.

"Anyhow, the chemist had trained some of our people. Walked them through the process. Things had gone well. The first batch was fire. Esmeralda wanted to celebrate, to show the chemist a good time while he was here in Iowa, so we all went out. Had an expensive dinner, then ended up at Toothless Romeo's. We were there for awhile, and picked up some entertainment before leaving."

"Romeo supplied the girls?"

"They're Esmeralda's girls, farm boy. Whether they know it or not. Romeo's just the face of the operation. So we took a few of em with us."

"This happen a lot?"

"I don't know what a lot means. Enough. They were always well-compensated."

"And Rosemary was one of the girls?"

"Yeah, it wasn't her first time. She was usually there."

"Why was that?"

"Esmeralda liked her. She had moxy. Men liked her. She'd do most things if it meant tweak."

"So you leave X's and O's—who was with you?"

"Me, Esmeralda, Toothless Romeo, the chemist, and the girls. Rosemary and another. Maybe two other. Can't remember. I do remember it was a pretty packed limo."

"And where'd you go?"

"Back to the compound outside Hegemony." Leon flicked the ashes from his cigarette into the cup. "We opened some wine, did some more of the new batch. We were just celebrating, you know? Queenie even had some propane tanks set up for target practice."

"Target practice?"

"Yeah, you never liked to blow shit up?"

"That really work?"

"If you duct tape a live flare to the side, yeah."

"So everyone was outside shooting propane tanks."

"Nah, just the three of us. Me and Queenie and Carlos, her main enforcer. She was the only one that managed to hit anything. Fucker lit up the whole sky."

"Where was everybody else?"

"They'd sectioned off. Romeo was doin' his thing with one of the girls. The chemist took a liking to Rosemary. He ended up comin' outside a little while after the explosion. That's how we found out she was gone. We searched the entire house for her. Thought she was just wiggin' out. Then Queenie realized the shit was missing from the dining room table."

"Rosemary stole the drugs?"

"Not all of it, no. Queenie never kept a substantial amount on the property. But it was enough to get someone a good chunk of change. Or really fuckin' whirly. But Queenie was livid."

"What'd she do?"

"Tracked her down, man. Sent out the forces. We found her running three miles down the road. She saw the headlights and darted into a field, but we just drove in after her. She was exhausted—panting and crying and whatever. Not that it mattered, but she wasn't thinking straight. We drove her back to the compound, and that's when . . . that's when Queenie killed her. Right there in front of the house. Strangled her with a piece of rope."

"So then you cut her up?"

"I didn't, but, yeah, Esmeralda had her dismembered. I just disposed of the bags." Exhaling a final puff, Leon put out his cigarette in the cup. "I'm just the bagman."

"Bagman that took out Randy Lee Wise and left a souvenir."

Leon smiled, slyly. "Not quite, but he got what he deserved. Mouthbreather was too big for his britches."

"And yet you're here just the same."

"Well, farm boy, how's it feel?"

"I've had worse days."

"You sit there resting on morality and law, but you're just like me. Just like all of us. Dirty hands. Only difference is that you hide 'em."

William held up his hands, palms toward Leon. "Doesn't look like I'm hiding anything. They look pretty clean to me."

"You crossed the line. Let me ask you something. No bullshit now. You kill for those duffle bags?"

"Little fat bird told me where they were. You're sloppy, Leon. Missed what was right in front of you."

"I knew it." Leon grimaced and backhanded the Styrofoam cup off the table. Water and cigarette ash splashed across the floor.

"Behave or I'll have to put the cuffs back on you."

"You think you really know what's goin' on here? You're missing what's right in front of *you*. You think Fry doesn't know about your proclivities?"

William stirred in his chair.

Leon chuckled. "'I have more respect for a man who lets me know where he stands, than the one who comes up like an angel and is nothing but a devil.'"

"I'm sure Malcolm would be proud."

"You smug bastard. Lemme clue you in. It wasn't me at the trailer." Leon paused. "Fry does freelance."

"Bullshit."

"Little happens in this town without Fry knowing. He's our little peacekeeper. Think about it."

"He take out Romeo?"

Leon smiled again. "Nah, that one was me. He and Tucky Fuck were making a move with some rubes. They took out the Grass brothers and lil' man."

"Rubes?"

"Dunno. Some wannabes. A guy named Robert Crimley and his flunkies. I'm sure there's a farm full of corpses out there by now."

"Where?"

"No idea."

William let his cigarette drop to the floor and stomped on it.

"Like I said . . . we're both dead men. In the end, I made the same play as Rosemary."

"Why?"

"Esmeralda was convinced things were just beginnin', but what was comin' felt more like the end to me. A hard rain." He smirked. "But just 'cuz you got 'Born to Lose' tattooed on your chest don't mean you don't go for it."

Outside the room, voices rose. William jumped from his chair and cracked the door. The unmistakable sound of gunfire caroomed inside the station.

"Shit," Leon said. "Looks like Queenie's come to collect."

William pulled his gun and slid from the interview room to the end of the hall. A cubicle blocked his line of sight into the main office area. He edged his head into the room a few inches and craned his neck up to see the convex mirror above the entry way. Widy and Darwin

Cash were dead at their desks. Farther back, near the station's entrance, a black-clad paramilitary held a gun to Sheriff Fry's head. Two more similarly dressed men flanked a woman.

It could only be Esmeralda Castillo.

"Leon's here," shouted William. "I'll kill him."

"Then Sheriff Fry takes one," Esmeralda hollered back.

Her man pushed the gun barrel harder into Sheriff Fry's temple.

William ran back to the interview room. He nabbed Leon by the crook of his arm and jerked him from the chair.

"Hey, what are you doin'?"

"Your lady's here for you."

"You can't—"

"I don't have a choice." William shoved the gun into Leon's ribs, pushed him out the door, and dragged him down the hall. He propped himself against the wall, wiped sweat from his forehead. "All right, I've got Leon. Let Hollis go."

"You first," Esmeralda replied.

He shoved Leon into the room. Leon walked meekly between cubicles, raising his hands. "Hey, love . . . I know things got fucked but—"

Esmeralda shot him twice in the stomach.

Leon staggered back and collapsed to the floor, blood blossoming on his shirt front. He laid his head on the tile with his eyes on the ceiling. "Fuck . . ." he said and he coughed up blood.

"William, they know you have the drugs. Just give em up," said Sheriff Fry.

"They're in my trunk."

"Toss out the keys," Esmeralda called.

William lobbed the keys into the room. They chimed against the floor and slid a few feet. William could still see them from his place at the wall. There was silence, and he peered up into the mirror again. Sheriff Fry was walking down the path between cubicles. He came into view a second later and then bent down to pick up the keys. He glanced over at William, gave him an unreadable look.

In the mirror, William watched the sheriff return to Esmeralda and hand her the keys. Another shot rang out—he couldn't make out who fired—and the sheriff dropped.

"Matarlo," Esmeralda said as she backed out the station's entrance.

The three enforcers marched forward.

William sprung from the wall and fired around the corner. It hit the first man in the throat. The other two responded with a storm of bullets from their assault rifles. William ducked behind the cubicle, chunks of corkboard and paper exploding from the wall behind him.

He leapt back into the hall. Past the interview room, the soles of his shoes slipped on the tile and his feet flew out from under him. He crashed down on his right elbow and smacked his head.

The men reached the hall and fired another burst. The barrage ricocheted off the concrete wall and tore holes in a mounted fire extinguisher. Releasing a cloud of carbon dioxide, the container shot to the ceiling and bounced back to the floor. White fog filled the hall as

William rounded the corner. He rushed to the fire door, kicked it open, and hurtled outside, coughing.

He ran to the parking lot and braced himself behind a group of squad cars. Seconds later, the men emerged from the smoke pouring from the door. They covered their mouths and fought back coughs. William leaned forward on the trunk of the squad and fired a shot into the one closest to him. The man disappeared into the smoke. The other lifted his weapon and released another shower that ripped paint and metal from the side of the squad. The windows shattered.

The man continued to fire as he marched toward the car. A bullet tore William's shoulder and he fell to his back. Lying on the pavement, he flipped to his side, crawled under the squad car and fired a round into the man's shin. The man buckled and William fired a second shot into his other shin. The man wailed and dropped to his knees.

William ended the man with a deathblow to the chest.

He wriggled out from under the car, and twisted onto his back, out of breath. A breeze wafted at his face and he stared up at the stars, thinking of nothing but his son.

29

Roland drooped forward, elbows on the bridge railing, and peered down into the river. The moon's reflection flickered in dark swirls, the water simultaneously still and unrelenting. Black oak and grass swayed in an intermittent wind, and he stood there for some time, trying not to think.

Thoughts came anyway.

Finally, he crossed the bridge and shuffled down to the river bank where an owl hooted from the shadows. He collected small rocks that soiled his palms and he whipped them into the water, one by one, each skipping along the choppy surface before disappearing in silence. When he had thrown so many stones that his hands became wet and muddy, he wiped them on his jeans and then sat down. It was getting colder and he zipped up his hoodie, tugged on the hood strings. He lit a cigarette and watched the water lap the bank.

Behind him, where the bank changed into an incline, Roland heard rustling in the grass. He turned, only half-interested, and saw the kid, the Mexican kid, hiking down to him.

"Hi," the kid said when he reached Roland.

Roland nodded, taking a drag from his cigarette and blowing it in the opposite direction of the kid.

"You don't have to do that," the kid said, nodding to the smoke. "My mom smokes. I already get it second hand."

"Right." Roland didn't speak for awhile, expecting the kid to move on. When he didn't, Roland said, "This isn't a place for a kid at night."

The kid shrugged. "I like it here."

"Right. Why you—Can I ask—How come you sleep down here?"

"I like the river. I feel safe here."

Roland nodded. "Me too. Say what you want about this—maybe this town's—but this river—it's just––I don't know anything as—there's nothing more beautiful."

He turned back to the river. The kid sat next to him. They stared at the glittering black in silence for some time.

"Well, I should get movin'," Roland said, standing up.

"You have to go?"

"Yeah—I got shit—there's a few things—I got business to attend to." Roland held out one of his mauled hands. "What'd you say your name was?"

The boy smiled and shook his hand. "Miguel."

"Roland. Good to—it's nice to meet you." He took back his hand and shoved it in his hoodie. "You—You take care—be careful out here."

"I can take care of myself."

"I'm sure you can."

Roland climbed the hill and didn't look back.

259

He crossed Foster on to Route 7, waiting for a car to pass, and walked up Logan two blocks to the Pump N Dump. Eugene was working behind the counter. He nodded to him, squinting from the change of light, and sauntered to the back to get a Dew. In the miscellaneous aisle, where they stocked toiletries, air fresheners, and other random over-priced items, Roland picked out a roll of duct tape.

"How you doin', Roland," Eugene said as Roland put the items on the counter.

"All right."

"Bit chilly out tonight. Gettin' to be that time of year."

"Yep." Roland paid for the Mountain Dew and the duct tape. "Gotta use your pisser."

"Sure. Go for it."

He walked to the restroom in back and locked the door. At the sink, he set the soda down, and he unreeled three long strips of tape, ripping each off the roll with his teeth and sticking them on the edge of the sink. Then he pulled the gun from his hoodie, and wrapped it into his palm with the three strips. It fit snug in his hand. Looked like a duct tape mitten. He slid his index finger, Polanski, over the trigger.

Perfect fit.

He left the bathroom, head down and hands shoved into his hoodie pockets.

"Stay warm out there," Eugene said as Roland pushed open the door to step outside. Roland simply nodded.

Two blocks later, he remembered he left his Dew in the restroom.

Along the way to the house, a strange wind blew through him. He felt outside himself, and time seemed to slow, and he descended as if from a great height, down through the leafless trees, and hovered above himself as he walked the sidewalk.

The bags of cans were still there when he wrenched open the screen door and stepped onto the porch. The TV bellowed from inside. He shuffled forward, and banged on the door with his taped hand, a great church bell tolling inside of him.

A few seconds later, Daniel Paul Bible ripped open the door with a sneer.

"I thought I told you—"

Roland leveled the gun, Polanski on the trigger, and fired a shot into Bible's gut. Bible staggered, reached out as Roland fired again, and then clenched his stomach and fell to floor. Roland stomped on him with a boot heel, sending Bible's teeth flying through the air, before retreating from the porch.

The TV was on in the living room, some late night talk show host trying very hard to be funny with a young Hollywood starlet. Roland's mother snored loudly in her recliner, the light from a lamp left on, a cigarette still burning in the ashtray. He grabbed the remote from the nightstand and clicked off the TV, put out the cigarette, and pulled her crocheted blanket up over her shoulders. She stirred for a moment. He thought she would wake. Then he bent down and kissed her on the forehead.

"Night, ma."

The cats greeted him when he stepped inside the kitchen—rubbed themselves on Roland's jeans, did circle eights between his legs, and scurried down the hall. Roland went to the fridge and dug out the last can of Mountain Dew.

Downstairs, in his room, he sat on the couch and cracked open the can. Emptied the soda in two gulps. Smoked a cigarette down to the filter. The duct taped hand was beginning to sweat and grow uncomfortable.

He stared at the wall for a long time.

He heard the door squeak open, heard her heels clap on the stairs as she came down. Just like they used to. She rounded the corner wearing a black dress, her skin pale as porcelain, her red hair pulled back into a ponytail that bobbed as she approached him. She draped her arm around Roland and whispered in his ear. Something he couldn't understand. Something he desperately wanted to understand.

He raised his taped hand toward his face, eased the barrel of the gun into his mouth. Polanski on the trigger. And then the shot and Roland left this world.

30

William stepped into the living room to find Lionel reading the newspaper from his recliner. He looked up and smiled.

"William," Lionel said, setting the paper to the side. "Good to see you. How's the shoulder?"

He got up from his seat, and hugged William. William embraced him for a long moment, and then said, "It's fine. A little sore, but I'm fine."

"I'm glad. I've been worried."

"It was just a flesh wound."

"Maybe, but I'm still your father."

"I know." William patted Lionel's shoulder.

His father sat back down. "Any leads on this woman?"

"No, none. A burning SUV on the shoulder of Route Thirteen. Her property's been seized, but she's gone."

"Shame. You think they'll find her?"

"Hard to say. She's well connected and has deep pockets. Suppose it's a matter of time. However long that might be."

"Couple nights ago, I had this dream." Lionel paused. "Woke up in a cornfield, the sound of cicadas buzzin' in my ear. I was looking for your mother. She was lost again. Across the cornfield, I saw her in her nightgown. Her back to me, moving in the other direction. I started to run to her. I was bookin', William. Whippin' through the corn. Thrashin' it. But no matter how fast I ran, I just couldn't reach her. The gap between us always remained the same.

"Then she vanished, pushed into the corn and was gone. I came to a clearing—a place where the corn had died and was fallen in a giant circle and the dirt was dry and cracking. I ran into the circle. There, in the center, black tar bubbled up from the earth. It started as a low gurgle and quickly got higher, shooting up into the air like a geyser, spraying the ground and me with black goo until I was drenched in it."

Lionel glanced out the living room window into the night, then he looked back on William.

William moved to the couch and sat down, closer to his father. With his good arm, he reached into his jacket. Pulled out the prescription bottle Roland had given him, and passed it to Lionel.

"What are these?"

"It's used to euthanize pets these days, but mixed with alcohol, it will put you to sleep. For good."

"Why would I need 'em?"

William inhaled. "For Sara."

Lionel's face stiffened. "Absolutely not."

William sighed, scratched his chin. "It's painless. She'll swig it down and close her eyes. It's that rapid. You could help ensure she has a peaceful death."

"No. I can't do it. I'm not ready to give up on her."

"You wouldn't be giving up on her. Besides, it should be about what's best for her."

"I'm done with this conversation." Lionel put the bottle on the coffee table and picked up his paper.

William sat there for a minute, rubbing his temple. Then he got up and strolled to Sara's room.

He could hear the sound of her breathing as he sat on the other side of the bed. He pulled back the blanket to see her face. Her head turned toward him and she opened her eyes.

"I'm sorry. I didn't mean to wake you. I just wanted to make sure you were all right."

She studied him like he was a stranger.

He got up to leave.

"Please don't go," she said. "If you go, I'll be all alone. I don't want to be alone." She held out her hand.

"It's okay—I'll stay with you until you fall back to sleep." He sat back down and took her hand.

She closed her eyes.

William parked the car on the shoulder of Foster Road. He picked up Roland's funeral card from the passenger seat. On the front was the Twenty-Third Psalm in cursive. He flipped it over to a picture of Mary with Roland's birth and death dates at the bottom.

Roland would have been horrified.

He put down the card and picked up the small cardboard box. Only a handful of people had been at the funeral. There had been himself, Roland's mother,

Delilah and Ray from the Rock Bottom, and three people William didn't recognize. The Reverend gave a short sermon and a man in a wheel chair played a rickety version of "Amazing Grace" on keyboard. After the service—when he had gotten up to leave—Sheryl had pulled him aside.

"Roland would have wanted you to have this," she had said, giving him the box.

He exited the car, box in hand, and walked to the bridge. A vigorous wind blew against his face, throwing his tie over his shoulder. Halfway across the bridge, he stopped and pulled back the tape on the box, his hair wildly unfurled in the wind. He stood there for a moment and waited for the wind to die down and then he released the ashes over the rail.

The remains fell from the box and spread out into the air like a great eagle gliding down into the dark waters below.

The elevator stopped at the seventh floor and William stepped out onto a zig zag patterned carpet. He walked down the hallway, studying the apartment numbers before coming to 705. He knocked on the door.

A man with a beard answered.

"Michael," William said. He extended his hand.

"William," Michael replied, shaking William's hand. "Come in."

Over Michael's shoulder, on the living room couch, William could see Angie. He nodded and took a few steps into the apartment.

"Joshua, your dad's here," Angie called.

There was the sound of little feet running and then Joshua shot into the room.

"Dad!" He ran to William at the door.

William bent down, scooped him up into his arms, and hugged his son tightly.

"You ready to go?"

"I am," William said.

"Don't forget your bag." Angie held out a small backpack. To William, she said, "There's his toothbrush and some clean clothes."

He set the boy down and Joshua ran over and slipped into the backpack.

"Okay, let's go, dad."

"All right." William smiled and glanced up at Michael and Angie. "We'll see you Sunday."

William closed the door behind them. He walked with Joshua back to the elevator.

"First, we can play with guys. I've got Batman and the Joker and some other guys. And I brought some Legos."

"You did?" William pushed the button for the elevator.

"Yeah, the ones you sent me—thanks, dad, I really like them—and we can stay up late and watch some movies and eat popcorn."

"We've got a busy weekend ahead of us."

Joshua looked up at William and smiled. "I know, right?"

The elevator dinged and the door slid open.

Snow fell outside the window. It was getting dark early now, but the sounds of the city never ceased. He'd been back for two months, and besides Joshua's room, most of his things were still in boxes.

William sat on the couch and pulled a box to him and ripped back the duct tape.

Inside were a few mugs wrapped in newspaper. Some bric-a-brac he didn't remember he had. Laying flat on the bottom of the box was the Occupants' LP *Shaky Hands*. He pulled it out and looked at the cover and then flipped it over. His eyes fell on Roland's name.

He got up and put the mugs away in the kitchen cabinets and returned to the living room. He looked at the record again.

For the next half hour, he searched for his old record player among the boxes. He finally found it in one marked 'clothes' and set it up on the living room floor. He took the Occupants' record from the sleeve and put it on the turntable.

It began to play with a warm pop and hiss.

To William's surprise, the first song was a fairly quiet acoustic number with psychedelic undertones. And even more surprising was that, according to the liner notes, Roland provided the vocal.

"All the clocks have stopped in the world," Roland sang. "And the sunshine pinched me. And for the first time, my grief got sleepy. And there was no one to be." Then it went into the chorus. "Forgive me, if this is all I'll ever know. Forgive me, if our grace comes slow."

William sat and listened to the album front to back, opening a window and smoking cigarettes from the couch in silence.

When it was over, he returned to the boxes.

In the one marked 'bathroom' he found a handful of prescription bottles. He took them out, one at a time, and looked at them. He came to one without a label, unscrewed the cap, and plucked a small baggie from the inside.

He stared at the powder inside. Then, abruptly, he stuffed it back into the bottle and tightened the lid. He put the bottle with the rest of the prescriptions and set the box on the floor.

He sat for some time staring at the wall, rubbed his temples. Finally, William stood from the couch, and strode to the bathroom to take a long hot shower.

He felt a migraine coming on.

j.thomas richards was born and raised in Rock Island, Il. He currently lives outside Iowa City, Ia. with his fiancée, teenage son, and three cats.

www.j-thomasrichards.com

twitter: @loosemeatnoose